THE
LITTLE
BLACK
DRESS

LINDA PALUND

Harmony Ink

Published by
Harmony Ink Press
5032 Capital Circle SW
Suite 2, PMB# 279
Tallahassee, FL 32305-7886
USA
publisher@harmonyinkpress.com
http://harmonyinkpress.com

The Little Black Dress
© 2014 Linda Palund.

Cover Art
© 2014 Cover Art by Anne Cain.
annecain.art@gmail.com
Cover content is for illustrative purposes only
and any person depicted on the cover is a model.

ISBN: 978-1-62798-851-3
Library ISBN: 978-1-62798-853-7
Digital ISBN: 978-1-62798-852-0

Printed in the United States of America
First Edition
May 2014

Library Edition
August 2014

I dedicate this book to my sister Judy,
whose little black dress left such a profound impression upon me.

ACKNOWLEDGMENT

THIS BOOK is based on a song I wrote on a dare. Someday, I hope to sing once again....

PROLOGUE
THE DREAM

I HAD that dream again. The one where Carmen was still alive. You would think I would know it by heart; I'd had it so often. Yet, in my dream, I was always surprised to find myself walking among the gray monuments that stuck up from the sand like stone teeth. I looked up at the graceful palm trees that cast their long shadows over the graves, and it all came rushing back to me. The faint scent of the ocean wafted above the tarry smells from the streets, and I knew I was at the Angeles Rosedale Cemetery. That's when I remembered that this was where they'd held Carmen's funeral.

But in my dream, Carmen was still alive, standing by her own graveside, the groves of palm trees forming a surreal backdrop behind her. She looked glorious, as usual, in her little black dress and spiky heels—the same outfit she wore when she was murdered; the same outfit she wore when they buried her.

Her mourners huddled together in the shade of the palm trees, whispering among themselves and staring down at her coffin, but I was not with them. I was alone on the other side of her grave, facing her. She was looking straight at me with an expression so forlorn it would have broken anyone's heart, but my heart was already broken.

I wanted to call out to her, but when I opened my mouth to shout, no sound came out. The world around me was deathly quiet, with a silence so profound it made my ears ring and filled me with dread. All I could do was gaze back at her from the other side of her grave and wonder.

Strangely, it was always daytime in my dream, with the bright sun of a Los Angeles spring day shining through the palm trees around me. But of course, it had been a day just like this when they held her funeral. The daylight kept my dream from being spooky in any traditional way. The horror I felt now was the horror that came with the knowledge that Carmen was really and truly dead, that her coffin was really down there, lying at the bottom of her grave, even though I could not bring myself to look at it. I only wanted to gaze at her beautiful face forever.

One of the most peculiar aspects of my dream was that, in real life, on the day of Carmen's funeral, I never actually made it to the gravesite. I couldn't face it. I stayed huddled alone in my car, weeping, until it was all over. I knew I couldn't endure the graveside speeches or the crowd of onlookers, and I certainly couldn't have endured the sight of her casket being lowered into her grave.

My dream of Carmen by the graveside haunted me in a way a ghost could never have, for I could not forget that desolate look in her eyes nor shake the feeling she was imploring me to do something. I couldn't be certain, but I figured she wanted me to find her killers. This was something I wanted to do with all that remained of my heart.

Still, I awoke from that dream with a start, shaken and terrified, in the way you do when you dream you were falling, as if I were falling into Carmen's grave.

CHAPTER 1
TEN MINUTES

IT ONLY took ten minutes. That was all. Ten minutes and our lives were changed forever.

It was Wednesday afternoon, and Carmen and I were supposed to meet after my tutoring session with Wendy, my dumb friend from down the block. She's the great dancer who was also incredibly stupid, but whose movie director father wanted her to get into a good college, so I tutored her in algebra in exchange for dancing lessons. She actually was an amazing dancer. She'd been taught by some of the best choreographers in Hollywood, and she had a natural talent for it anyway.

The plan was for me to meet up with Carmen after I finished with Wendy, and then we'd drive down to Santa Monica and visit our favorite hangout, Shakespeare's. We already had a cover story worked out. We told our moms we were going to work on our world history project at the Santa Monica library, which everyone knows is open late on Wednesday nights.

But it was April and a beautiful spring day. It made Carmen feel restless. She told me that the afternoon was so lovely, she would walk down the hill and meet me at 6:00 p.m. on the corner next to that famous old telephone booth, the one where Frank Sinatra Jr. telephoned his dad for his ransom when he was kidnapped back in the sixties. That was a pretty sad story, but this one was sadder.

She rang me on her cell at ten minutes to six. "Hey, it's me." She had a rich contralto voice with just the slightest trace of a Southern accent. It would be impossible not to know it was her, especially as her smiling face flashed up over her name on my cell phone screen. "Are you almost ready? I'm leaving now and heading down the hill. You won't be late now, will you?" And she laughed her sultry, musical laugh, because she knew I couldn't wait to get away from Wendy.

She also knew Wendy would be listening to my side of the conversation, so when I said, "Don't worry, I won't be late," she knew I meant it.

So at 6:00 p.m. on the dot, I said good-bye to Wendy, hopped into my little red Mazda, and scooted down the hill to the corner and pulled up beside the empty telephone booth. But Carmen was nowhere in sight. There was a low guardrail around the small parking area that we always sat on when we had to wait out there, but no one was sitting there now. There was no one around at all. All I could see was the scrub brush and the empty telephone booth, and all I could hear was the sound the cars made on the 405 freeway nearby, a sound like the ocean. I called Carmen's name, just for the hell of it, but my voice was lost in the smog and the sound from the freeway. No one answered.

I called her cell, but it went straight to voice mail. That was odd, I thought, but maybe she was talking to her mom or something. I texted her and then gave myself five minutes before I tried calling again. It was the longest five minutes I'd ever spent. I sat on the guardrail and listened to the traffic and stared at my phone, praying for it to ring. I watched the clock slowly tick over; then I dialed Carmen's number. "Pick up, pick up, pick up," I kept saying, but it went straight to voice mail again. I left a message anyway. "Hi, Carmen, where are you? I'm down at the phone booth. Call me back!"

Then I rang Wendy, just in case we had our wires crossed somehow, and Carmen had stopped at Wendy's instead. Wendy picked up right away, completely surprised by my call. "Hi, Lucy, did you forget something?"

"Oh, I was wondering if Carmen showed up at your house." I tried not to sound concerned.

"Wasn't she going to meet you at the phone booth?"

"Yes, she was, but she's not here yet, so I thought maybe she stopped by your house on the way down."

"No, she's not here. She probably got held up by her mom or something. I'll call you if she shows up here."

No, I thought to myself, of course Carmen wouldn't be there, but where was she?

I called her home phone. Her mom picked up after about ten rings, already three sheets to the wind.

"Hi, Mrs. Caruso, is Carmen there?"

"No, dear, isn't she with you?"

"No, she was going to meet me down on the corner by the phone booth, but I guess she's just late. I thought she might still be at your house."

"She left here fifteen minutes ago."

That was when I really got worried. "Oh well, I guess she must have stopped to talk to somebody. Bye, then." I said cheerfully and hung up, but I was overcome with fear.

There had to be something wrong. Carmen and I had met at this phone booth countless times. Where could she be? I suddenly felt as if my heart was on fire, and my lungs forgot how to breathe. I walked around the little parking area in front of the guardrail and scanned the brush along its edges, but I didn't see anything. Everything seemed peaceful and ordinary. A warm breeze carried the drone of the traffic, but nothing else, nothing that would explain where Carmen was.

I got back into my car and drove slowly up the hill, calling and texting Carmen the whole way and searching the hedges and lawns of every house I passed. There was no sign of her. She had disappeared. It took all my strength to keep from crying, but I decided to go straight to her house, just in case something weird had happened and she'd gone back home for something she'd forgotten. Maybe she had left her phone in the bathroom. That was possible.

I zoomed into their driveway, scrambled out of the car, and ran through their little gate and up the steps. Mrs. Caruso answered the door before I had even pressed the doorbell. She looked mystified, but I could see she was beginning to sober up.

"Has Carmen come back?"

"No, honey, I'm sure I would have heard her." She held the door open, and I walked into their familiar foyer. "I don't understand, dear. She's always with you."

"I don't understand either, but maybe she came back for something, and you didn't hear her come in. Have you looked in her room?" I started running down the hall to Carmen's room, yelling her name, with Angela following close behind. I burst into her room. "Carmen?"

But her room was empty, her bed made tidily with its mauve-and-black comforter. I checked her bathroom, but she wasn't there either.

"Oh, honey, she's not here. There's no one else in the house at all."

Angela sat on the edge of Carmen's bed and watched me as I tried calling her cell phone again. Once more, it went straight to voice mail, and this time I knew for certain something was really wrong.

I found out later they had thrown her cell phone out of the window almost as soon as they had her in the car. The police would find it a week later in a ditch full of old Coke cans and used hypodermic needles about half a mile from the telephone booth.

My fear must have gotten through to Angela, because she suddenly laid her head in her hands and started to cry. "My poor child, my poor child...," she kept repeating over and over.

"We have to call the police," I told her. "I'm going to do it now." And I stood by the bed and called 911—my mom had made me set it on speed-dial in my phone. It took me a while to get through to the right department. And then it took me a while to get through to the idiots on the end of the phone. They didn't believe it was an emergency. I had to get Angela to speak to them, to convince them this wasn't a schoolgirl prank, that this was a completely out-of-the-ordinary situation, and it didn't look good.

They finally put her through to Missing Persons, but the officer Angela spoke to said there was nothing they could do right then, that we would have to wait for twenty-four hours before they could file a missing persons report. Angela hung up the phone, and we looked at each other in disbelief. We both knew waiting was useless.

I sat down on Carmen's bed next to Angela. Then I called my mom. She was home, thank God, and she picked up right away. "What's the matter, Lucy? You sound like you've been crying."

"I think something has happened to Carmen. She was supposed to meet me down at the phone booth after I finished at Wendy's, but she's not there, and she's not answering her phone either."

"She's probably gone back home for something. Don't worry."

"No, she hasn't. I'm there now. With Angela. She's not here either. She isn't anywhere. We called the police, but they say there's nothing they can do. We have to wait for twenty-four hours before they'll even file a report. I'm so worried." I began to cry again. "Will you come over here now? We need you."

"Oh, of course I will. I'll be right over."

My mom was a shrink. Maybe she would have some magic words that would make all this worry go away. All I knew was that I didn't want to leave Carmen's house. And who knows? Maybe my mom could come up with a plan. She knew how to handle cops. Maybe she could get them to take us seriously.

Angela stood up then, swaying a little, and walked to the door, more slowly than I had ever seen her walk. "Well, I had better put the kettle on," she said, "if we're going to have company." As if this was going to be just a pleasant social call.

Even then, I knew something terrible had happened to Carmen, and there wasn't going to be a happy ending. I could feel it in my stomach and I could feel it in my heart.

There was an exit from the 405 freeway that came pretty close to that corner where the telephone booth was. Anyone could have seen Carmen standing there in her little black dress. She would have looked like an easy target. She *was* an easy target.

I stayed where I was, sitting on Carmen's bed, and I took another long look at all her things, her jewelry lying in neat little bowls on the dressing table, the photograph from our dance recital pinned up next to the film poster from *Mulholland Drive*. I breathed in deeply, just to get the scent of her inside me; then I stood up and followed Angela down the hall. But all the while, my heart was beating so slowly I thought it might just stop. I wanted it to stop, but it kept on beating anyway.

CHAPTER 2
THE NEW NEIGHBOR

MY SORRY teenage life began to blossom the summer before my sixteenth birthday, when Carmen moved into the house across the street from me. That house had been on the market for months, and I had waited in terror to find out who would finally be moving in. Then, one Saturday, I noticed a new gardener clipping the hedge, and when the realtor arrived on Monday to remove the FOR SALE sign, I scampered across the street to give her the third degree before she had time to scrape the dirt off the stake and pack it away into the back of her Lexus.

"Hi there," I said. "I see you finally sold the house."

The realtor lady was probably feeling pretty flush from the sale because she looked up and smiled at me and began to boast.

"It really wasn't on the market that long, and it was a cash sale. The new owners will be moving in soon."

My heart jumped a little at that. "Oh? Gee, do you know anything about them?" I was hoping to hear a nice family from some sophisticated place like New York City would be moving in and that they had a daughter my age.

The lady realtor just smiled again and opened the car door, but before she slid into her seat, she said something that would throw me into a stew of euphoria and anxiety for the next several weeks. "Well, honey, it looks like you're in luck. A family from Virginia bought the house, and I am pretty certain they have a daughter about your age." Then she backed out of the drive and headed up the hill, leaving me staring at her chrome tailpipe with my heart beating a little bit faster.

Still, it was nearly a month before the moving vans started rolling up and our housekeeper, Constanza, called me to our spying station behind the blinds over the kitchen sink.

"Miss Lucy, the trucks are here!" she whispered gleefully, pulling apart the blinds so we could get a better view.

I was giddy with hope, but as anxious as I was, I couldn't have known then how truly special my new neighbor would turn out to be or how important she would be to my life. All I knew then was that I couldn't wait to meet her.

Later that evening, after the moving vans had gone, the family finally arrived in a taxi, but the mother hustled her daughter into the house so swiftly, I could only catch a glimpse of her face, a flash of pale skin surrounded by a mass of dark hair. But there was enough light to see she was wearing one of those little black dresses that hardly reached to the middle of her thighs and showed off how long and shapely her legs were and the kind of spiky high heels my mom would never even let me try on. Then the door shut behind them, the taxi drove away, and that was that.

The neighborhood I lived in was located in West Los Angeles, California, a little island of wealth between Wilshire and Sunset boulevards. It was one of those neighborhoods where the houses weren't quite grand enough for movie or rock stars to live in, so their lawyers, therapists, or yoga instructors lived there instead. We even had the movie stars' rabbi living in our neighborhood. I know, because I used to have to play croquet with the rabbi's daughter every Sunday afternoon. It was that kind of neighborhood.

My house was at the top of our hill, but just down the hill from us lived the movie director, whose daughter, Wendy, introduced me to the Sugar Shack on Sunset Strip. Next door to me was one of those rock stars' lawyers. He had two sons. The younger son was my little brother's best friend. Up around the bend lived an artist who designed album covers. His son was an artist too. His name was Steve, and I was pretty certain he was gay. He hung around with the rock star lawyer's oldest son, Sam. They were the ones who'd introduced me to Shakespeare's in Santa Monica, which became my favorite hangout.

Even though the house across the street probably sold for a mint, it wasn't really that spectacular. It was a hybrid of New England colonial and Hollywood-style ranch house constructed of white-painted clapboard, with green shutters purely for decoration and surrounded by a low white picket fence with a hedge behind it. The house was about a mile long but only one story high. It should be noted that the house once had the title role in a movie called *Mr. Blandings Builds His Dream House*. A sweet older couple, retired from the wardrobe department at 20th Century Fox, had made it their dream house until they suddenly packed up and moved to a retirement village near San Diego last April.

The day after the new family's arrival, my mom had the bright idea to have Constanza bake some of her special Mexican chocolate spice cookies so I could have an excuse to go over to the new girl's house. I didn't even know her name yet. I didn't know anything about her at all. But when the cookies had cooled sufficiently and Constanza had put them on one of our fancy cookie platters and covered them with plastic wrap, there was nothing for me to do but break the ice.

In the meantime, I had spent the morning perfecting my makeup and trying on about half a dozen outfits until I found one that didn't make me look fat: tight jeans and a long black stretchy top, which I accessorized with lots of silver chains and big hoop earrings. I wore a pair of wedge sandals, as close as my mom let me come to high heels.

I summoned all my courage and traipsed across our road and up her walk, holding tightly to Constanza's tray and trying not to stumble. I rang the doorbell, which was one of those chiming doorbells that played a tune so old I couldn't recognize it, and within seconds, there was the new mom, all made up and dressed like she was about to step out onto the set of *Dallas*.

"Well, hello, y'all," she drawled, and by that I mean she had a gorgeously lilting Southern accent. That was when I knew for certain she wasn't from around here. That and her hairstyle. Her glossy blonde hair was done up in the kind of coiffure that called for at least a can of firm-hold hairspray to hold it in place.

"Why, are those for us?" she asked, smiling a toothpaste-advert smile and looking for all the world like the mother in *Leave It to Beaver*, that fifties sitcom they still run on the Nickelodeon channel.

"Yes," I answered, grinning brightly and hoping she would invite me in. "My mom baked these for you to welcome you to the neighborhood," I lied.

"Well, isn't that just the sweetest thing," she said. "Why don't you come on in?" And she held the door open and made a sweeping gesture to point me in the direction of what I assumed was the living room, and that's when I clocked that she was drunk.

I found myself in their vestibule, which was much like the one at my own house, only theirs was full of enormous cardboard packing crates, and I had to navigate around these to find the hallway—which, if I followed the mom's pointing fingers, complete with crimson nail polish and what I thought were several real diamond rings, was through the left-hand doorway with the sham pillars painted on the walls. So I turned in that direction and headed down the hall, padding carefully around the piled-up boxes until I came upon one of those big double doorways that usually signaled an important room, and sure enough, they opened into a grand room with actual furniture in it, already set about in a cozy living room sort of fashion. Big fat sofas and overstuffed easy chairs and coffee tables and lamps and what you would expect in a living room. Except for the stacks of boxes piled against the walls, it was pretty much ready to be lived in.

We had a living room at our house, of course, but we never actually *lived* in it. It was strictly for formal occasions, special guests, and cocktail parties, and was kept shut up most of the year. We used the family room, which we called the den, to watch TV with the adults, and we had a "rumpus room" on the kids' level (it was a split-level steel-and-glass wonder my dad had designed with some famous architect) where we watched TV and my brother played those boy-type computer games. Our living room had classy black-and-white furniture and included an ebony grand piano and a fantastic stereo system that only got to be played on holidays. Anyway, here was a real living room, big and inviting, with a huge brick fireplace on one wall and all that lovely soft furniture waiting to be sat upon.

"Now, just you make yourself comfortable, sweetie, sit anywhere you like, and I'll see if Carmen can come out to meet you." And she swept out of the room, tipsy but graceful, while I set the platter down on a coffee table and made myself comfortable on a plump red-and-white striped sofa. Then I stared around the room and pondered the name Carmen.

So that was her name. How dramatic and how fitting, I thought, remembering the vision of thick dark hair and pale skin. But my reverie was short-lived. The mother came back into the room *without* her daughter.

"Oh, I'm so sorry, darling," she drawled, "my Carmen's not at all well. The move just took too much out of her." And she sort of fell back into one of the armchairs and smiled brightly at the cookie plate.

"Now, let's just try one of these," she said politely, sitting up and looking relatively alert. She pulled back a corner of the cellophane and picked out the smallest cookie on the plate. She took a delicate bite and exclaimed, "Oh my goodness, these are simply delicious! I must get your mother's recipe!" And she put the cookie down beside the platter and beamed her gorgeous smile at me and never touched it again.

"Where are my manners? I don't think we have been properly introduced. My name is Angela Caruso, but you can call me Angela." As soon as she said her name, all I could think about was her daughter's name, "Carmen Caruso." Such a beautiful name, almost musical, and so much more glamorous than mine.

"Oh," I said, smiling politely back at her. "My name is Lucy. Lucy Linsky, I live right across the street."

"Oh, you live in that spectacular house with all the glass and decking!" she marveled.

"Yes," I answered. "My dad's Dr. Linsky. He's a heart surgeon, and my mom's a psychiatrist. I've got a younger brother too."

"How nice." And she leaned across the table and looked at me wistfully. "Poor Carmen's daddy has just died, and we've come out here to make a new start." Then she sat up again and added brightly, "I have a son too, Carmen's older brother, James, but he's not with us right now. He's at the academy in Virginia."

"Oh, that's too bad. I mean about your husband... and your son... it's too bad that I can't meet him yet," I added, not knowing exactly how to respond to this news, "but actually, I was just wondering what grade Carmen would be in. I saw her when you moved in yesterday, and she looked like she might be about my age."

Mrs. Caruso clapped her hands and made with the toothpaste smile again. "Oh, just how old are you, darlin'?"

"I'll be sixteen in August, and I'll be in the eleventh grade. I'm a sophomore," I answered.

"Now, isn't that just ducky," Angela exclaimed. "Carmen will be sixteen in July! And she'll be in the eleventh grade just like you. I just know you two are going to be the best of friends!"

"Gee, I hope so," I said, cringing at how lame that sounded, but all the while I couldn't stop myself from getting excited about the prospect. There wasn't one person in the neighborhood and hardly anyone in the school I could relate to, and here was someone I just knew was going to be special, living right across the street from me. I don't know how I knew this, and I certainly didn't know then whatever it was that made her so special was what would also make her so tragic.

CHAPTER 3
MORE THAN FRIENDS

IT WAS to be several anxious days before I finally met Carmen. I kept my eye on her house all the while, though, hoping for another glimpse of her, but all I ever saw was her mom going in and out carrying bags of groceries or bottles of booze, it was hard to tell which. Various delivery people and workmen rang the bell, but the door was never answered by anyone but her mom. And then one day, a few weeks after they moved in, when I had actually begun to give up hope of ever meeting her, our doorbell rang. My little brother Jeffrey ran to answer it, and a few seconds later, he came running wild-eyed down the stairs to report that some amazing-looking girl was at the front door asking for me.

It was summer, so I was dressed casually in cutoff jeans and a T-shirt, but this being LA, I grabbed a quick peek in my bedroom mirror and touched up my eyeliner before trotting up the stairs to meet her.

No matter what I had imagined her to be like in person, seeing her in the flesh was another experience altogether. There she was, standing outside my front door, holding that same cookie platter I had brought over to her house and looking back at me with luminous brown eyes with eyelashes I swear were about a mile long. But it was the way she was standing that was so awesome: she was so completely composed, so totally nonchalant and sure of herself, I knew she was absolutely aware of the impression she was making.

She was dressed in a little black dress that clung to her body as if it were painted on, and her thick dark hair framed her perfect heart-shaped face. I could feel myself becoming more shy and awkward with every second I looked at her until she suddenly flashed this brilliant smile at me, a smile so amazing I was immediately lost in it, lost in the warm sparkle of her sturdy white teeth and the most delicious dimples I had ever seen.

I tried not to show how astonishing I thought she looked, and I mustered a casual "Hello," which she answered with a husky "Hello" back, and I invited her in. That was all there was to it. We deposited the platter in the kitchen, and I brought her downstairs to the rumpus room, where I introduced her to my nerdy but eager brother, then took her into my bedroom and showed her my laptop and my collection of indie-weird music, and in one afternoon, she became part of my life forever. When she wasn't hanging out at my house, listening to my music, or watching my DVDs, I would be over at her house, listening to her music and watching her DVDs.

We were like twins separated at birth. We shared nearly everything, and what we didn't already know, we accepted and learned to love. She turned me onto Sylvia Plath, and I had her reading Shirley Jackson. We ravaged each other's libraries and lay on our backs on our beds in my bedroom or hers, reading out loud to each other from F. Scott Fitzgerald.

There was no doubt in my mind she was special. She was charismatic and beautiful enough to be a movie star, but all she wanted to be was a poet. That was a hugely wondrous ambition for a young girl and slotted into my life perfectly, as I planned to be a novelist. But where I had only written a few short stories at that time, mostly school assignments, Carmen already had a collection of astonishing poetry, all of it exquisitely dark.

We lived like no other teenage girls in Bel Air, and we took great pride in that fact. All that summer, we made a point of never going to the beach or visiting a mall. Everything we wanted, from books to cosmetics, we ordered from Amazon or downloaded from the Internet. We created a bubble in which we could live like the artists we dreamed we were: intense, intellectual, and beautiful. There were only a handful of places we would leave our bubble for, like the NuArt cinema, where we went to watch foreign films or weird old retrospectives. And then there was Shakespeare's and The Sugar Shack.

Shakespeare's was this retro coffee house in the basement beneath an acoustic instrument store in Santa Monica. It was owned by a couple of older ex-hippie gay guys, Sebastian and Cedric. They welcomed anyone who wanted to hang out there, no questions asked. It seemed to be open all day long and had the ambiance of a cavern, with lots of little café tables with candles and chessboards or *Dungeons & Dragons* game boards on them. There was a giant espresso machine on the counter and a kitchen that seemed to serve only coffee and brownies. Bookshelves lined every wall except the one where they had put up a small stage.

Shakespeare's had its share of nerdy college students playing chess all day and several obvious runaways, gay or otherwise, who seemed to live there all the time. It was kind of a misfits' retreat, and I immediately felt at home there from the moment I trotted down the rickety staircase.

Cedric was working the counter that day. He was an extraordinarily handsome black man, who, for some reason, maybe because it was LA, always walked around barefoot. He had amazing-looking feet. I didn't know what the health department would make of them, but as long as they didn't bust him, I didn't care. His brown eyes lit up when he saw us, and he greeted us with his usual welcoming grin, his gigantic teeth gleaming in the dim light as he came around from behind the espresso machine.

"Hi, Lucy," he said. "Who's your friend?"

"This is Carmen," I answered. "Carmen, this is Cedric. He owns the place with his partner Sebastian."

"Cool," said Carmen, looking around, taking in the dark cavernous space with its candlelit tables, the walls covered in bookshelves, and the unusual clientele. There were still some kids sleeping on benches in the back, and a skinny boy was sitting on a stool in the farthest corner, strumming a guitar and singing mournfully. Several of the tables had young couples sitting at them, talking in low voices, some of them holding hands. Most of these couples were boys, but I noticed Cathy and Linda were there, sipping coffee and looking into each other's eyes. By the door, two boys I didn't recognize sat together, their arms around each other, and one of them had his head lying on the other's shoulder. "Cool," she repeated, squeezing my hand.

"So, you're new here, aren't you?" asked Cedric. "I detect an accent."

"You got me, y'all," Carmen drawled delightfully. "From Virginia. I've been in LA for exactly four weeks, but I like it here already."

"I see that Lucy is bringing you to all the best places," he said, walking back behind the counter. "Can I get you anything to drink?"

"Coffee would be very cool," answered Carmen. I just stood beside her and beamed happily at Cedric, who obviously approved of her.

"You take it black like Lucy?"

"Oh no. I take it sweet and white," she answered. "Can you make me a latte?"

"Oh yes, pretty one. Sweet and white for the pretty little lady, coming right up."

I led Carmen to the table closest to the counter. I usually sat at the counter when I came to Shakespeare's because I liked to chat with Sebastian and Cedric. That was also because I always came by myself. This was the very first time I had brought anyone with me. I knew most of the regulars, though, like Cathy and Linda, but a lot of kids drifted in and out, following the runaway route up to San Francisco through Walnut Creek and on up to Portland, Oregon.

It was a curious bit of synchronicity that led to my discovery of Shakespeare's. A few years ago, just when I was entering my first year as a teenager and my last year as a junior high school student, I dropped by our next-door neighbor's house to fetch my little brother home for dinner.

Sam was the older brother, and he hung out a lot with Steve, the album artist's son from around the corner. They were a lot older than I was, so I never had much to do with them, but I liked them all right. I could tell they were different from most of the other high school boys I'd seen. I thought that was because they were both sort of artsy types. "Artsy type" was a label I gave myself. They had working parents like us, and the kids had been mainly brought up by their housekeeper, Portia, who was the coolest black woman you could ever hope to meet, so being right next door, I liked to spend time over at their house, just to listen to her talk.

As usual, Sam's parents weren't home, and Portia was fixing them dinner. The two older boys were sitting on the deck just outside the kitchen, chatting and drinking that strange adult beverage called coffee.

"Hey, Lucy," Sam said. "Come sit down for a while. Leave the boys alone a little longer. Let them finish their big Xbox tournament downstairs."

I was impressed Sam even remembered my name.

"You know Steve, don't you?" he asked.

"Of course," I answered.

"Well, come on, then. Sit down. Have a cup of coffee."

"I don't drink coffee."

"Of course you do," he said, smiling charmingly. Sam was tall and lean, with very curly sandy-colored hair that never seemed to be in any particular style. He had deep blue eyes and a narrow, lightly freckled face with quite an impressive nose and a good smile that made his eyes sparkle.

His friend Steve had been a surfer, or maybe he still was. He had that bleached-blond surfer hair with bangs that hung down over his forehead and nearly covered his green eyes, making him look both boyish and mysterious. He wore this kind of knowing grin, which made him seem a bit arrogant, but he'd always been nice to me.

"Portia? Could you bring another cup of coffee for Lucy?" Sam called through the screen door.

"Here, Miss Lucy," Portia said, a moment later, putting a mug of black coffee down in front of me.

There was nothing for me to do but take a sip. It tasted awful, hot and bitter, but drinking it made me felt terribly sophisticated.

"Sam tells me you're an aspiring writer," Steve said.

"Well, I like to write," I answered, taken by surprise.

"Don't be shy, Lucy," Sam said. "Lucy has won all the writing contests they have at Emerson Junior High, haven't you, Lucy?"

I was amazed Sam knew this, but I guess my little brother must have bragged to Sam's little brother.

"Well, that's really saying more about the caliber of creative writing in the rest of the student body," I answered.

"I told you not to be shy about it. I read your last story from that contest in March," he said. "I showed it to Steve too."

My face must have gone totally red. "You did? Why?"

"Steve is organizing a writers evening at Shakespeare's."

"What's Shakespeare's?" I asked.

"That's a hangout we go to in Santa Monica," said Sam. "You'd like it too. You don't have to be over eighteen to go there. They don't serve alcohol, so it's an all-ages kind of club."

"It's like a beatnik coffee house from the fifties," Steve added.

"Anyone can go there and just be themselves," said Sam. "It's open twenty-four hours a day. We thought you might like to check it out."

"You did?"

"Yeah, we did," Sam said. "Steve's putting together a group where aspiring writers, like yourself, can meet up and read short stories out loud to each other, like a poetry reading night."

"You should totally come down and check it out," said Steve.

"Totally," agreed Sam.

I didn't drive then, of course, and I wasn't going to take the bus, so my mom drove me to Shakespeare's the following Wednesday night. Embarrassingly, she insisted on coming inside the club with me.

"This is amazing," she said as we made our way furtively down the steep steps. "I swear, I might have been here back in the sixties!"

It was pretty dark down there, and it took me a while to realize most of the people hanging out there were gay couples. That's when it finally occurred to me that Sam and Steve were gay. Then it dawned on me that they must have thought I was gay too!

I sat there with my mom for the whole night, sipping drinks and listening to some pretty good short stories. Steve was the moderator, or whatever they call the guy who introduces the readers. He always had a kind word to say about each person's story, and when it was over, he came and sat down at our table and chatted to my mother and me.

"Next week, Lucy's going to read a story, aren't you, girl?" he announced to my mom.

"Oh yes, absolutely," she said.

"I don't know. I've never read any of my stories out loud." I tried to back out, but my mom wasn't having any of it.

"Come on, Lucy," she said. "You're in drama class. You give readings all the time. And you played the rabbit in *Winnie the Pooh* last year. I know you're not shy!"

"Mom!" God, was that embarrassing. "All right, I'll do it, but please stop talking about me, okay?" I begged.

"Great," Steve said. "See you next week, then." He was about to get up, but then he thought of something else to ask. "Hey, so what do you think of this place?"

"It does seem really cool," I said. "My mom thinks she may have been here back in the sixties."

"She might well have been. It used to be open back then too. And remember, Lucy, it's open all day, so you can just come here and hang out after school. It's not that far away."

"Yes, Lucy," my mom said. "This might be a good place to meet some interesting friends."

So that got me thinking. Did even my mom think I was gay? Was I *really* gay? And if I was, was I the last one to know? Did everybody else just assume I was gay? Okay, I had suspected it for some time. Probably since I was twelve years old, but I had never really thought about it, about my sexual orientation, I mean. That's probably because I was a late bloomer. I hadn't even had my first period yet. But I'd always known about sex. In fact, I knew *a lot* about sex.

Being a shrink, my mother had a huge library of psychosexual pathology books upstairs in her office, and by the time I was eleven years old, I'd read every book from Havelock Ellis to the Kinsey Reports. She also had a collection of what she called "dirty books," which were really some old pornography like *The Story of O* and *Candy*, which she hid under her mattress. Most of these made sex seem pretty ugly and were filled with a lot of male aggression. Everything about sex in them was hard and hurried and seemed pretty painful to me. But I liked the descriptions of the women, with their sweet-smelling voluptuous bodies and silken skin. Everything soft and warm and curvy was womanly, and I discovered, at the age of eleven, that it turned me on.

Then, when I was twelve years old, I found some *Penthouse* magazines in a neighbor's recycling bin while I was walking to Westwood Village. I took them and hid them in my shopping bag. I couldn't wait to look at them, and I opened one up inside the ladies' room at the first coffee shop I came to as soon as I reached the Village. The sight of all that naked womanly flesh made me feel strange and tingly and also very itchy, so that I had to rub my crotch with my fingers. That felt so good, I reached my first climax in the toilet stall at Coffee Island. It felt so weird and wonderful; I couldn't wait to do it again.

After that, I began to masturbate pretty much every day, sometimes just thinking about women and sometimes using the magazines I'd found. Then I began to read some of the other books in my mom's library—psych books about sexual orientation—until gradually I began to get a picture of what might be in store for me. But I wasn't ready to accept it. I was a kid. What did I know?

But after that night at Shakespeare's, I kind of liked the idea that I was different. I mean, I had always known I was different from the other kids in my class, but now I knew I was even more different than I had originally thought. I was more than a geek. I was queer. I was a lesbian. But of course I wasn't going to tell anybody. That is, until the day I walked into Shakespeare's with Carmen.

Cedric brought us our coffee, smiling from ear to ear, just like the cat that swallowed the canary, but he left us alone after that. As soon as he had disappeared behind the counter, Carmen took one sip of her latte. Then she put it down on the table and cocked her beautiful head to one side and looked at me with a quizzical expression on her face. It was an expression I had never seen on her face before, and I feared the worst. Then she said it.

"So, are you gay?"

I wasn't exactly startled, but I put down my own mug and looked back at her with kind of a half smile on my face, trying to collect my thoughts and figure out exactly what I was going to say. I had been planning this for days, but now my heart was beating like a tiny frightened bird trying to escape my rib cage. I didn't know what to say. We were already so close. In the three weeks since she'd appeared on my doorstep, we'd been practically inseparable. We had slept in each other's beds. We had tried on each other's clothes and stayed up 'til all hours of the night listening to The Cure's *Disintegration* album. We had shared a lot of secrets, but this was a secret on a whole other level, and I knew it. I took another sip of my coffee. It suddenly tasted as bitter and awful as it had the first time I'd tasted it over at Sam's house.

"I don't know," I answered, nervously fingering the handle of my mug. I looked up at Carmen again, wishing I could read her mind. "What about you?"

Carmen took another sip of her latte and sat back in her chair and simply gazed back at me, not smiling, but not frowning either. Her beautiful full lips were drawn tight, but her eyes shone in the glow of our little café candle.

"I don't know either. I never thought about it until I met you," she said, totally surprising me and making my heart flutter, as if the bird in my chest was about to break free.

That's when I reached across the table and took her hand again.

"Let's not worry about it," I said. "Let's just be friends."

She smiled then and shook her head, her lush hair swirling about her shoulders like it always did. "Don't be silly, Lucy. We're already past that." And then she did something really strange. She lifted my hand to her mouth, and she kissed the back of it, a wet kiss, so that I could feel the tip of her tongue against my skin. The touch of her tongue was like an electric shock that I could feel all the way through my body, from the tips of my breasts to the tips of my toes. If I had had any doubts before, I was certain now. I really was gay. And what's more, I was in love with Carmen.

From that day forward, Shakespeare's was our home away from home. We tried to make it down every Wednesday night too, for the short story and poetry readings, and we took turns contributing our efforts. But mainly it was a refuge where we could cuddle in public and kind of show off our relationship. Otherwise, we felt like we had to hide it, although I am pretty certain my mother knew. I guess it was our peers we feared, and I know Carmen was afraid to upset her tipsy mother.

On weekend nights, though, we usually went dancing at the Sugar Shack on Sunset Strip. They didn't play that eighties disco crap or that awful manufactured R & B drivel everybody else seemed to like. They didn't serve any alcohol either, but they sold a lot of Red Bull and JD Orange and Passion Fruit drinks. It was at the Sugar Shack that we got most of our exercise.

Carmen was a dreamy dancer. I mean that literally. She danced as if she was asleep or on drugs, just dreamily graceful, every movement slow but in perfect time—as if she could make time stop. If I were asked to describe her dancing, I guess that would be my description: she danced in a way that seemed to make time stop. I had my own repertoire of fabulous Wendy-the-dancer moves, but I learned a lot from watching Carmen dance. Like how to dance as if you could stop time.

If only I could really do that. Stop time, I mean. Then I could go back and save Carmen from her fate.

CHAPTER 4
THE LITTLE BLACK DRESS

OUR RELATIONSHIP stayed strong even after school began in the fall. In a town like LA, this was a major accomplishment. My high school had all the usual bullshit every other high school had with its cliques and gossip, but multiply this by the duplicity and back-stabbing endemic to LA, and you realized it was nothing less than a miracle we could keep our friendship so solid.

We also had to get past the issue of the little black dress. This was a mystery that took me a long time to unravel. At first I didn't notice, because during the summer at home, Carmen wore all kinds of summery outfits every day, just as you would expect any good-looking teenage girl to wear: light gauzy dresses that made you gasp when you looked at her, shorts that clung to her round bottom and showed off her legs, and halter tops that barely covered her astonishing breasts. But whenever we went out, whether to the cinema, to the Sugar Shack, or even to Shakespeare's, Carmen only wore one thing: her little black dress.

She accessorized like crazy, though—beads and bangles, gold or silver necklaces, jet beads or rhinestones, fantastic earrings, hoops or drops, diaphanous scarves and wide belts, but always, always, the little black dress.

So I wasn't exactly surprised, on the first day of school, to see her prance down the walk in her four-inch heels, looking like a million bucks but wearing that same little black dress. I don't know what I expected, but I hadn't really thought she would wear that dress to school. I remained bewildered that she kept right on wearing it every single day, but I was too good a friend to make an issue of it. If that little black dress was destined to become her high school uniform, so be it.

It turned out that was exactly what it was, for I am not exaggerating. She wore it every single day of the school week. Of course I wondered about it, but I didn't dare ask Carmen why she wore it. I don't know why, but somehow I knew this subject was taboo. We shared so many things, but this was obviously something she wasn't ready to share with me.

I thought about it a lot, though. Finally, I came to the conclusion the dress must have something to do with her father. After all, he had just died that year. Maybe in Virginia, the teenage girls had to dress in mourning for a whole year. But then, it also seemed especially weird to me that neither Carmen nor her mother ever spoke about her father, and I never saw a photograph of him anywhere in the house. They didn't really seem to miss him. Still, maybe she actually was in mourning, and maybe that was the only black dress she owned. All I knew was that, every single day when we would meet up in front of one of our houses to drive to school together, there she would be, looking fetching, looking ravishing, looking gorgeous, but always in her little black dress.

I'm sure I wasn't the only one. I'm sure everyone at school wondered about that dress. This was LA, after all, the town where even five-year-olds had their hair done every two weeks and their noses done by the time they were eight. If you didn't buy your designer clothes on Rodeo Drive in Beverly Hills, you bought their knockoffs at Marshalls in Santa Monica. You simply did not go to high school wearing the same dress every day. But nevertheless, that is what Carmen did. The same exact dress, every single school day.

So, yes, I wondered about that dress a lot. I wondered about practical things too, like how the hell did she keep it looking so fresh? Did she wash it by hand every night? I even wondered if she had more than one of the exact same dress. But what I really wanted to know was, what was its significance? What did it mean to Carmen?

Anyway, after a few months, I finally got up the courage to ask her about the dress. That was a mistake, though, believe me, and I was so sorry I brought it up, but I couldn't help myself.

We were downstairs at my house, in the rumpus room, eating the popcorn Constanza had made for us and watching *Gone with the Wind* on DVD.

I had been planning to ask her for weeks, and I thought I had worked out my best plan of attack. After all, we were relaxed now, we'd seen the film before and we both loved it, so we could talk during it, making comments all through the film, and I could practice my Southern accent. But now I tried my very best to be subtle as well as casual.

"Hey," I said, keeping my eyes focused on the screen, watching Scarlet cavort in her ragged gown after the Yankees had destroyed her beloved Tara. "I've been meaning to ask you." Then I took a deep breath and tried to look as cute and casual as I could when I finally asked, "Why *do* you wear that same dress to school every day?"

Carmen froze for a second in the middle of reaching for a handful of popcorn. Then she turned to me with a look of shock and fury. And there was something else too. Something close to rage was flaring up behind her eyes. But all she said was "I can't believe you're asking me that!" Then she threw down the big yellow bowl, so that the popcorn spilled all over the couch, and she stormed up the stairs and out of the house, slamming the door behind her.

I sat there numbly for a few minutes, staring at the TV screen, watching Scarlett O'Hara turn her drapes into a ball gown, and then I cleared up the popcorn, switched off the TV, and went to bed.

There were so many things I didn't know about Carmen. So many subjects I had to steer clear of. We liked so many of the same things—the same books, the same movies, the same TV shows, and the same music— but there was still a huge part of her I feared I would never get to know.

I was hopelessly in love with her. It may have been a schoolgirl crush, it may have been puppy love, but it was some kind of love. I loved her, and I didn't want to ruin our friendship. So I went to bed early that night and fretted and worried so much I couldn't sleep, and finally I had to sneak upstairs and steal a Valium from my mother's medicine cabinet. She was out playing bridge, and my dad was working late as usual, so I was safe. Then I went back to bed and slept like the dead until my alarm woke me.

The next morning, Carmen was outside my house at 8:00 a.m. as usual, leaning against my car and looking up at the perpetual blue of our autumn skies, acting like nothing had happened and nothing had changed. She was wearing her little black dress as always, with her amazingly lustrous hair piled on her head so just a few ringlets fell about her neck, making her look deliciously disheveled.

"Hey," she said like she always said when she saw me, her face breaking into her wicked smile, her adorable dimples lighting up her face.

"Hey, yourself," I answered, practically stumbling down the walk with my arms full of books, trying to gauge her expression to determine if she was really all right.

"Here, let me help you, silly. Ever hear of a book bag?" She took the top three books off my pile so I was able to click the opener for the car door locks, and we managed to dump the books into the backseat. Her book bag was lying on the ground by her feet. It was a retro shoulder bag we had found in Venice, and it had a picture of David Bowie from the *Heroes* album on the flap. I never did find one for me, and I was damned if I was going to use my old backpack.

We were up close and personal now, bending over the car, our arms entangled in books and our hips touching, when she surprised me by putting her arm around me and giving me a reassuring squeeze. Then she surprised me even more by giving me a little peck on the cheek.

"So, we're good?" she asked.

"Better than good," I replied, straightening up and smiling back at her dimpled cheeks and bright eyes. I breathed a sigh of relief, wanting desperately to kiss her but knowing that was something we could never do in public.

Then she shrugged her shoulders, picked up her book bag, threw it into the backseat on top of my books, and climbed elegantly into the passenger seat, her little black dress riding up almost all the way to her crotch. We were carpooling, and it was my turn to drive. It was all I could do to keep my hands on the wheel and not slide one hand up between her beautiful thighs, but that was all she ever said about last night, and I never dared ask her about that dress ever again.

CHAPTER 5
THE DEAD FATHER

BECAUSE CARMEN was so damned beautiful, she was exempt from any of the usual harassment high school cliques subjected most kids to, including me. Everybody wanted to be her friend, but she was surprisingly unpretentious and always cool, never giving away too much but just enough to be desired by everyone. I basked in the light of her favor and in the fact that she still gave me most of her attention, and everyone knew we were best friends, so I became cool by proxy—and that was all right with me.

She was at least as smart as I was, so we were in all the advanced placement classes together, and then we really lucked out that year because we were allowed to take modern dance instead of team sports, so PE wasn't the hell it had always been in the past. Dance class made us look even more cool, so we were about as cool as you could get in high school without being a cheerleader.

Carmen's biggest problem was her attractiveness. Even with wearing the same damn dress every day, she attracted unwanted attention, attention from the teachers for being so smart and pretty, and attention from boys for being so damn sexy. But the Jocks were by far the worst of them.

High school boys in LA could pretty well be broken down into four groups: the Jocks, the Surfers, the Nerds, and the Hopeless Geeks.

The Jocks were all the sporty guys—the guys who were actually good at sports. The Surfers didn't give a shit about anything but the surf. The Nerds were the smart guys who were totally uncool no matter how cute they might be, because they weren't Surfers or Jocks, but they pretended not to care. And the Geeks, well, they were the poor pathetic ones even we could ignore.

My little brother was a total nerd, but he really *didn't* care.

It had become perfectly clear to me, almost from day one, that Carmen, no matter how gorgeous she was, no matter how sexy she looked in that little black dress with her wavy black hair swirling around her lovely shoulders and her thousands of brightly colored bangles jangling around her slender wrists, had a thing about boys. Preferring girls as sexual partners was one thing, but it seemed to me she bore a great antipathy toward the entire male sex that verged on hatred.

She tried not to let it show, but I could see it, a deep rage that boiled beneath her beautiful surface every time a guy tried to make contact with her. Usually she smiled a totally fake but effervescent smile and put them in their place in such a sly and beguiling way they didn't even know they had been put down.

I wanted to ask her what all this rage was about, but now I knew better. It made me wonder about her father. Actually, I wondered a lot about her father. I was afraid to ask Carmen herself, so I tried to ask her mother, but all I ever got out of her was a lot of drunken sighing, accompanied by incoherent comments like "Oh no, dear. He's dead, and that's the end of it. It's so very sad…," and then she would stagger off to the liquor cabinet for a pick-me-up.

I finally got my chance at Christmas, when Carmen's older brother James came home. All this time he had been at a military academy in Virginia, but now I finally got to meet him, and happily, I liked him right away. I could see he was truly fond of Carmen, and she was truly fond of him.

He was awesomely polite, very Southern gentlemanly, and very soldierly. I was hanging out over there a lot, so I was there on Christmas Eve. Angela was drunk as a skunk as usual, but charmingly so. We were all drinking eggnog, but Carmen refused to have any alcohol in hers. I guess the example of her dipsomaniac mother turned her off to drinking, but I thought it was fun—and it warmed me up and made me feel totally comfortable. They had a fire going in the living room and an unbelievably tall tree her brother James had brought home on the top of his car.

By midnight, Angela had stumbled off to bed, and I could see Carmen was bored and wanted to go to bed too. She was signaling me to come along with her for a little cuddle before I went home, but I pretended not to notice and just sat in front of the fire with James, sipping my eleventh eggnog until Carmen shook her stunning head and called good night before trouncing off to bed.

I wasn't attracted to James or anything. He was just Carmen's older brother, and I wanted to be alone with him so I could ask him about his father. He didn't look anything like Carmen, but I guess he looked a bit like Angela. He was blond, which made me realize Angela's hair was probably really blonde too, and not bleached as I had assumed. He was kind of thick around the middle, not very fit for a soldier, but I guess he was one of those nerdy kinds of soldiers. I think he was studying intelligence or "intel," they called it.

I waited until I was absolutely certain Carmen was far away in her back bedroom, and then I began, speaking as quietly and as casually as I could. "You know, no one here ever talks about your father," I said, choosing my words carefully. "I'm sorry if I'm out of line, but can you tell me anything about him at all? Whatever happened to him? How did he die?"

James just looked at me for a few moments. I could see he was startled by my question, but he was too polite not to answer. He took another sip from his glass and said simply, "Well, they think he committed suicide."

"They *think* he committed suicide? Don't they know?"

"Well. It wasn't all that clear. He was out on a hunting trip with some friends. They were the ones who found him, but it turned out that he was shot with his own handgun."

"Oh, that must have been awful for you," I said, horrified.

"Yes. It was pretty awful," James said, strangely calm. He stared into the fire, then turned to look at me. "It was really awful for my mom."

In for penny, in for a pound, I thought. "Is that when she started drinking?"

James surprised me by laughing ruefully. "Oh no, that had started long before Dad died."

"Do you miss him?" I asked.

James turned back to the fire. He put his glass down on the coffee table and leaned forward to pick up the fireplace poker. He began to poke at the logs until the top one burst into flames with a roar, and the sudden heat warmed my face. Then he sat back, chewing on his lower lip. "No. I wouldn't say that exactly, but I will tell you he was one hell of a father." He nodded at the fire and kept biting his lower lip. "One hell of a father," he repeated. He stood up then and looked down at me. "I left home as soon as I could. I sent myself to military school!" And he gave a grim little laugh.

"He was that bad?" I asked. Now we were getting to it. I had always wondered why there weren't any pictures of Carmen's dad in the house. Now I desperately wanted to know more, but James was turning to go.

"Yes. He was that bad," he said finally, turning to look at me again, not even trying to smile. "I was selfish. I should never have left them alone with him." And then he was at the door, and I was getting up, and I knew I wouldn't learn anything more that night, but then he turned back to me and whispered, "Please don't tell Carmen I told you anything about him." I nodded and he added, "Don't tell anyone, will you promise?"

"Of course. Of course," I said. "I'm so sorry that I brought it up… I just wondered… and no one would tell me anything…."

James was such a gentleman; he had quickly brought me my coat from behind the front door and held it for me while I slipped it on.

"Don't worry," I assured him as we walked down the hall. "I won't say anything. I'll see you all tomorrow with your Christmas presents," I added, changing the subject.

James opened the front door and watched to make sure I made it safely across the street to my own darkened house. I turned and waved after I found my key and opened the door. Then I went straight to the medicine cabinet and got out two aspirin. I would have a terrific hangover tomorrow if I wasn't careful, but it was worth it. I felt that much closer to understanding some of the mystery surrounding my beloved Carmen.

CHAPTER 6
THE ABYSS

IT TOOK them three days to find Carmen's body after we reported her missing that April afternoon. It had already been the worst three days in my life, but with the discovery of her body, I felt as if the world had simply opened up and dropped me into an abyss so deep I would never be able to crawl out of it.

Highway workers uncovered her body lying in a drainage ditch behind the Stop & Shop off the Pacific Coast Highway in Malibu. The creeps had tossed her body from the car or van or whatever they'd used on the very night they took her. Maybe I should have been thankful she'd been killed the night they took her and that she hadn't had to suffer too long.

The police had been interviewing me every day since Carmen disappeared, wanting to know everything about her, who she hung out with, who she dated. I was in a fog through most of it, thanks to my mom's Valium, which she was feeding me for breakfast. I had stopped eating and was living on Red Bull. Fortunately, I was able to mumble the same answers over and over, because the answers to their questions were simple: Carmen spent nearly every waking moment with me.

They still went ahead and interviewed Carmen's teachers and classmates. With their usual police-academy tunnel vision, they just assumed she'd run off with a boyfriend. It was only after they found her brutalized corpse that they considered she had actually been abducted.

Then the interviews started all over again. I must have gone over those ten minutes about five thousand times. I had nothing new to offer them, and they had nothing new to offer me. What I really wanted was to know what had happened to her. However gruesome it was, I needed to know exactly what had happened to Carmen in those ten minutes and what happened to her once she'd been abducted, but the police wouldn't tell me anything. I was too young to be given access to any details of the autopsy, and I wasn't allowed at the inquest. All I knew was what I heard on the news like everyone else.

What they told the public was that there had been three perpetrators, and that's all they would say. They told Angela privately that they knew this because they had found three different specimens of DNA on Carmen's body and clothes, but these wouldn't be much help because none of the guys' DNA was in the system. They also collected some fibers from clothing and some hairs that could belong to the perpetrators, but nothing to match them to either. One bit of helpful information was that the hairs belonged to Caucasians. They took some hair samples from me to rule me out of the mix they had collected. They also took a sample of my DNA for the same reason.

Forensics also had fibers from the upholstery inside the vehicle, but these turned out to be a generic upholstery fiber found in most high-end utility and off-road vehicles, like SUVs or sports vehicles, although this seemed to be their biggest clue. It narrowed down the list to maybe one hundred thousand in the Los Angeles area. They didn't seem to have much else to go on, and it didn't look like they would ever catch the creeps who killed her.

Carmen's brother James had flown home as soon as he heard she was missing, and now he was staying with his mom across the street. I would stumble over there at least once a day, trying to be supportive and to ask if they had heard anything new, but we were all so shell-shocked we weren't really much comfort for each other, and poor Angela could only go through the motions of her usual Southern hospitality. Once we had determined none of us knew anything more, all we could say to each other was "Why?" And after that, I think we each wanted to be alone to weep. I am not convinced grief likes company. The police kept stopping by, though, to ask more useless questions—and they took some DNA from James too, but he didn't mind. We were all willing to do anything to help.

Carmen had been wearing her little black dress when they took her, so after the police had gotten all the evidence they could from it, they gave it back to her mom. Angela cleaned it and then sewed it up in the places that had been ripped and torn. It was practically in shreds when she got it back, but she fixed it up nicely, and when they released Carmen's body, she brought it to the funeral parlor, and they dressed Carmen up in it for her funeral.

Angela asked me if I wanted to come with them to pick out the casket, but I told her I couldn't face it. The existence of Carmen's coffin was an impossibility I could not reconcile. After all, there shouldn't be a coffin because Carmen shouldn't be dead. She should be with me, dancing at the Sugar Shack. She shouldn't be dead and lying in a coffin.

I couldn't come to grips with it. It didn't seem right or fair that I was never going to see her again. I couldn't face the fact that there was going to be a funeral. Then James told me it was going to be an open casket, and somehow that made me feel better. I was not sure why, but even though I knew in my heart she was really dead and she wasn't in her body anymore, I wanted to see her again. I *needed* to see her again.

Carmen's funeral was being held at the Angelus Rosedale Cemetery in Santa Monica, the one near the beach filled with palm trees. Everyone from our class would be there along with loads of press. It was now a famous "unsolved murder of a schoolgirl" case, and it had caught the public's attention. They had already started issuing warnings on television and radio advising all young women not to leave their houses without a buddy or to even cross the street alone.

Angela had arranged a private viewing just for close friends and family the morning before the "public funeral." Her relatives who had flown out from the East Coast would be there, as would James and I, along with my parents.

I was glad to have James there. He met us at the entrance to the funeral home and offered to walk me over to the open casket. It was the first time I had ever been inside a funeral home, but I had seen every episode of *Six Feet Under*, so I knew what to expect. All the same, this would be the first time I had ever seen a real dead body, and not just any dead body; it was Carmen.

As he escorted me up to the dais, all I could do was hold on to his arm for dear life and keep looking straight ahead, staring at the back of one of Carmen's aunts. She was wearing an expensive-looking hat, and I kept wondering if I should have worn a hat too.

Then suddenly, there we were, standing beside the coffin. James kept trying to turn me around so I would look at her, but even after all those episodes of *Six Feet Under*, it took all my nerve to turn and face her. I think I must have closed my eyes, finally, and when I opened them, there she was, laid out for all the world to see, looking so beautiful and special, dressed in her little black dress, wearing her silver necklaces and bangles on her wrists. Her eyes were closed, but her lashes were still as long and as black as ever, her lips as full and perfectly shaped. But her dimples were gone. She would never smile that wicked smile of hers again. Her lovely face was frozen and dead. She didn't look like she was sleeping. She looked like she was dead.

Those creeps had just picked her up and used her up and thrown her dead body into a ditch like a sack of garbage. They had taken her life. How could they have done that? She was so young and beautiful, and we had our whole lives ahead of us, and now she would never share mine again. At that moment, I didn't care if I broke down in front of everyone. I stared at her beautiful dead face and held on to James's hand so hard my fingernails dug into his palm until he finally squealed, and I had to let him go. I stumbled out of the chapel and found myself under a palm tree, and I leaned against it and sobbed.

I didn't notice my mother had followed me out. She was standing by another tree, watching me. No one was allowed outside without a buddy anymore. Then some woman came up to me with a little tape recorder and a microphone and a cameraman behind her.

"You're her best friend, Lucy, aren't you?" she asked me. "I wonder if you could just tell us something about Carmen...."

I looked up at her through my tears and shouted, "Just find them! Find them!" and my mother stepped in and told them where to go.

CHAPTER 7
THE HAUNTING

THE HAUNTING phenomenon started almost immediately after Carmen's murder, when Easter vacation ended and classes began again. I missed the beginning of this strange interlude because I didn't go back to school with everyone else after the Easter break. It had been agreed between the school counsellor and my mother that I should stay home and take as long as I needed to grieve.

But staying at home turned out not to be such a good idea. I spent my days in a stupor of depression and my nights in a Valium-induced trance, my moods vacillating between a catatonic numbness and an inconsolable sorrow. My staying at home meant that every time I looked out our front windows or walked out our front door, I would be confronted by her house. It would always be there, right across the street, a constant reminder that she would never be returning to it; I would never see her clattering down her front walk, wearing her groovy high-heeled shoes, and smiling at me with her wicked smile.

Something that really frustrated me was my terrible need to speak to Carmen. I wanted to talk to her about her murder and how badly it was affecting me. I wanted to tell her about her funeral and about her casket and how I couldn't face any of the details surrounding her death. These were the sorts of things we could discuss. I needed to talk to her about everything. But mainly, I needed to talk to her about the fact that she was dead. It was a paradox I could not reconcile and could not bear to live with.

The only respite I had from my despair was sleep, and sleep was hard to come by without my mother's Valium, so I pretty much continued to live on it. I had given up coffee and Red Bull so I could sleep, but I didn't know if it was the Valium or the valerian tea I was drinking, but I began to experience wonderful dreams: sweet dreams, not nightmares at all, about Carmen.

My dreams always began with me walking down the stairs to our rumpus room. Everything would be normal, and I would expect to see Carmen sitting on the couch watching a DVD like always, and sure enough, there she was, just the same as ever, stretched out on the sofa in her little black dress. She would look up and smile as soon as she heard my feet on the stairs, and by the time I reached the bottom step, she would be standing up and walking toward me.

We would meet in the middle of the room and then, as naturally as can be, we would hug. Just hug. We would hold each other close so that I would feel her cheek against my cheek and the warmth of her body against mine, and an overwhelming feeling of comfort and peace would surround us. I felt so at home in her arms, as if we were one person. And I remember thinking, if only this feeling could last forever. But then I would wake up, and a terrible loneliness would descend upon me, and I would know I was really alone, and Carmen was gone forever, and I would never hold her like that again.

So after a few weeks of total despair, I decided I might as well go back to school and try filling my head with something else. I had already heard some of the stories circulating around the campus from Wendy. Wendy had been extremely sweet and sympathetic during these weeks and kept appearing at my house every afternoon with offerings of junk food or some specialty her maid Delia had cooked up to entice me into eating again. I could never summon any appetite, but I appreciated the effort she made. She kept up a cheerful chatter about events on campus that buzzed around my head somewhere but never connected, but when she began to tell me the stories circulating about Carmen's ghost, I began to listen. At first I didn't believe something like this could actually be happening, and it only made me angry. I dismissed it as an "instant urban myth," and I was totally appalled something like this could arise out of something so real and tragic as Carmen's death.

When I finally returned to school, the tales of the "beautiful but vengeful ghost" who stalked the halls of Uni High had become pretty well established. Sightings of Carmen's ghost had become the talk of the lunchroom, so after a few days back, I figured I better find out what was really going on.

It seemed to have started with what I would call aural hallucinations. Boys reported hearing the sound of footsteps, high-heeled shoes tapping down the tile floors of the school's corridors. The sound would always seem to be coming from just ahead of them, just around the next corner, or just behind them, but when they turned around, there was nobody there, and if they ran to catch up and see what was around the next corner, there was never anyone there either. All the boys said it sounded exactly like Carmen striding down the hall in her high-heeled shoes and little black dress.

Then, about a week after I started back at school, I was called in to the vice principal's office. The vice principal was in charge of discipline in the school, and I, Lucy Linsky, had never in all my career at Uni High been called in to his office. So it was with curiosity as well as trepidation that I approached the administration's receptionist and asked why I had been summoned.

The vice principal came out to greet me and took me into his office, all solemn and solicitous the way all the teachers had been treating me lately. He asked me how I was doing and actually pulled out a chair for me to sit on. Then he got to the point.

"Lucy," he began, looking very serious and directing an accusatory gaze my way, "I wonder if you have heard the rumors that have been going around the school recently."

"What rumors would those be?" I asked, feigning innocence.

He put his elbows on the desk and rested his chin on his knuckles and looked at me with a steady gaze. "Several of the boys on campus have been reporting strange noises near the boys' locker room. They seem to think the school is haunted."

I just sat there and looked at him as if he was crazy.

"I'm not saying that the school *is* haunted, I am just telling you what some of the reports are that I've been hearing," he said.

"What kind of noises are they hearing that makes them think the school is haunted?" I asked, still playing innocent. "Rattling chains?"

"No, actually, the boys are reporting the sound of high-heeled shoes following them down the hallway. They say they have that peculiar echoing ring that Carmen's shoes always made. You don't know anything about that, do you?"

"Excuse me," I said, truly mystified now, "are you thinking I have something to do with those noises?"

"Well, I know you have a friend whose father is a film director. I thought you might be playing some kind of trick, using his help?" He looked at me accusingly again, and I could not believe what I was hearing.

"You really think I would have anything to do with that?" I was furious now. "I would never do anything like that. I would never do anything that might injure Carmen's memory for me. Never!" I was on my feet now, almost crying.

He must have believed me, because he backtracked pretty quickly and apologized mightily, and I left his office more perplexed than ever. How could this be happening?

Then the sightings began. Boys started reporting actually seeing Carmen—or who they thought might be Carmen. They reported seeing a beautiful girl walking down the hall a little way in front of them. She was wearing high-heeled shoes and a little black dress, and she was always only a little bit ahead, just out of reach. For some reason, they couldn't resist trying to catch up to her. But every time they got close, she would turn a corner, and when they followed her, she would vanish in the blink of an eye.

They all seemed to find this terrifying, and most of them would turn and run away as fast as they could. These sightings were reported so often it seemed to be some form of male hysteria. At least that's what James and I concluded. After my experience with the vice principal, I began to discuss the phenomenon with James. I needed someone to confide in, someone who knew Carmen and had an IQ that would enable them to see past the common perceptions.

James and I had started hanging out at Pips Coffee Shop in Westwood Village. It had a parking lot that was easy to use and served endless cups of coffee. It also had pretty good cheesecake, and if you ever went there for breakfast, it had these cool toasters on each table, where you could make your own toast, which meant yours would never get cold. Anyway, I liked it there. It made me feel grown-up to sit there sipping black coffee and talking to James, who already seemed pretty grown-up to me.

"Well, I'm no psychologist, but it sounds like some kind of mass 'male hysteria,'" James suggested over a big slice of Black Forest cake. "Have you seen or heard anything yourself?"

"No, I haven't," I answered. "And that's the weird part. If there was such a thing as ghosts and Carmen was one, wouldn't you think she would appear to me, of all people?"

"Yeah, or even to me." James agreed. "You say most of the sightings are around the boys' locker room?" He looked perplexed, and he frowned at his forkful of cake before it disappeared into his mouth. He had a strangely feminine mouth, with small, soft-looking pink lips, the opposite of

Carmen's mouth, whose lips were full and shapely. In fact, he was almost the complete opposite of Carmen in every way. He had a round face and small, very blue eyes. He wore his blond hair short, probably because he was at a military academy, but he still didn't look like a soldier. He looked like what he was: a gentle young man and my friend.

"Wendy and I were thinking that maybe jocks are more susceptible to this kind of hysteria," I said, driving thoughts of Carmen out of my head and trying to concentrate on her ghost. "We've tried hanging out near the locker room, pretending we were on hall patrol so as not to act suspicious, but neither of us have seen or heard anything."

"Maybe it's just a hoax," James suggested, "to keep nerds out of the boys' locker room."

"You would think so," I said, watching the waitress refill my mug for the umpteenth time, "but it's actually the jocks themselves who are getting scared. In fact, they seem downright terrified!"

James and I went over and over it, but the more we discussed it, the more incomprehensible it seemed.

I was still angry about Carmen's death and overwhelmingly sad. I could not imagine there would ever be a time when I could get over it. I was angry at the universe, and I was angry at the police for not finding her killers, but mostly I was consumed by the fiercest anger for the creeps who had done this to Carmen.

It was my own anger that led me to gradually believe in the possibility that Carmen could be haunting the school. After all, in a universe as perverse as this one, where someone as beautiful and special as Carmen could be murdered and have to spend the last hours of her life on earth being tortured and abused in such a horrific way, anything could be possible. Why wouldn't her young soul come back to haunt the rest of us?

If I was angry, she must be furious. I had seen her fury before, and I knew she held an unfathomable depth of rage inside her, and now? After what they had put her through? Her rage must have been monumental. I could believe she would be out for revenge, and it looked as if she was going to take her fury out on the boys at my school, especially the jocks.

I wondered about that.

CHAPTER 8
JONNY FREEMAN

THINGS ESCALATED with the strange case of Jonny Freeman. Jonny Freeman was one of the popular kids in our school, but he had a particularly unpleasant notoriety among the female population. He was an incredibly hot-looking guy, very handsome and very rich. He wasn't particularly smart, so he wasn't in any of my classes, but he was one of the "in crowd," the crème de la crème of the fashionable elite, and hung out with the hottest of the jocks, the captain of the football team, Luke "Skywalker" Ritter, even though he didn't play football. Jonny had earned his letter in track.

I had seen Jonny around campus, always surrounded by his cool buddies, and I had heard a lot of the gossip about him, usually from behind the stalls in the girls' bathroom. Stories about how he kept a running score on his phone that would text all his buddies automatically whenever he made another of his so-called conquests.

His so-called conquests were really just date rapes, which happened to be one of my pet peeves. I kept reading about these idiots who didn't believe date rape exists. They were usually men with no daughters or boys with no sisters, because everyone else knew it was real, and it was creepy and it was very, very wrong.

Anyway, Jonny Freeman was infamous for his disgusting dating behavior, what even the boys liked to call "scoring at any cost." His reputation was so bad that only a girl new to the school or one who had a very large older brother living in town or one who was foolish enough to think he wouldn't try it out on her, would go out with him. His tactics were always the same. He would invite some pretty and clueless young girl for a date. Just a dinner date, he would say, to get to know her. He would be smooth and charming, and he was cute as hell, so he was hard to resist.

He would pick her up at her house in his fancy Lotus sports car with the top down and take her to one of those "in" places on Melrose for dinner and sweet talk her all night. Then, on the drive home, he would take a little detour up Mulholland Drive. Mulholland Drive was not just a movie. It was an incredibly long and winding road that went over nearly every mountain pass and through every canyon and overlook in LA between the Hollywood Bowl and the town of Encino. Miles and miles long—and very steep, winding, and treacherous!

He would drive way up Mulholland Drive, so far up the girl would become suspicious and say she had to get home now. But he would laugh and smile charmingly and tell her there was this terrific view he was taking her to, it was such a beautiful night, she shouldn't miss it. And he would pull in to this secluded overlook where there was truly an outstanding view with Hollywood all lit up beneath her, and it would take her breath away and be oh-so-romantic, and soon he would be kissing her, and the next minute he would be pinning her arms behind her back and tearing her clothes off.

Now, some girls were happy to get it on with a hot guy from the in crowd on their first date—and that was fine, but if you weren't one of these and you would prefer *not* to get it on with Jonny Freeman on your first date, it didn't matter one bit to Jonny, because he was going to have you anyway, and he didn't care whether you wanted to or not.

If you were one of the few who managed to fight him off and get yourself out of the car, you knew you would be facing several miles of deserted road and would have to make it down in your high-heeled shoes. That prospect wasn't so attractive either, so a lot of girls just gave in to him to save themselves the terrifying walk home. But a few girls managed to fight him off and were willing to hobble down the hill carrying their shoes. The rest let themselves be raped and kept their mouths shut because Jonny Freeman was in the most elite clique in the school and there was no way anyone was going to touch him.

Of course, a few of the girls did tell, which was how even I, someone who was not a member of any crowd, in or out, knew, because it turned out that Wendy was one of the girls who'd hobbled home carrying her shoes.

I was lying on my bed reading Ayn Rand's *Atlas Shrugged*, because I was naïve enough to believe it was worth reading, when I heard this strange scratching sound. I got out of bed to investigate. The sound was coming from outside my back windows, and I realized somebody was scratching on my window screen. For a moment, I was scared, but then I remembered that when we were kids, Wendy and I used to sneak into each other's bedrooms in the middle of the night. We'd creep down into each other's backyards and scratch on the screens until one or the other of us would open the window and pop out the screen so we could climb right into each other's houses without our parents being the wiser.

Sure enough, when I opened the drapes, there was Wendy, standing outside my window and trying to keep the top of her dress up while holding her shoes in one hand and scratching on my screen with the other. I opened the window immediately and popped out the screen. She threw her shoes over the windowsill and climbed right in.

She looked a mess. Her feet were bloody, and her knees were scraped and bleeding, and her pretty green dress was ripped right down the front. I'm sure that dress cost a mint too.

"What happened to you?" I asked.

"Shh," she whispered right away. "I don't want anyone to know I'm here."

"Don't worry. My folks are in bed on the other side of the house. But what's going on? What happened? You look like you've been raped!"

She collapsed on my little sofa then and started crying. "I'm an idiot," she said through her sobs. "I went out with Jonny Freeman."

"You didn't!" I said. "Why did you do that?"

"I don't know. I don't know," she repeated. "I think I was flattered or something. He only asks out the really pretty girls. I thought there was nothing he could do to me. That, you know, I thought I could handle him."

"Oh, Wendy," I said and sat down on the sofa next to her and put my arms around her. "You poor thing. What did he do? He didn't rape you, did he?"

"No, he didn't, but not for want of trying."

"But what happened? What happened to your dress?"

"I'm just lucky I got away." Wendy shook her head and looked down at her torn dress. Then she looked up at me. "He's a lot stronger than he looks."

"Tell me what happened."

Wendy leaned her head back against the sofa and took a deep breath. She was still trying to cover her breasts with her torn dress, but she had stopped crying now and just looked at me with swollen blue eyes.

"He took me to this really nice restaurant. The one my dad's always talking about. The Ivy. He seemed sweet. I mean he acted sweet. He treated me like a real date." She shook her head as if she couldn't believe anything she was saying. "He asked me all about my dancing and didn't ask me about my dad, like everyone else always does. It was nice, and the dinner was lush."

"And then?"

"After dinner, we got back in his car, and I assumed he would just take me home. We were driving down Sunset Boulevard, and before I knew it, he turned the car, and we were heading up Mulholland Drive! I told him right away that he had to stop and take me home, but he just laughed and kept on driving." Wendy looked at me with angry red-rimmed eyes. "I thought about jumping out of the car, but he was driving so fast, I didn't dare. I started yelling at him to stop the car. Do you know what he said? He told me to shut up and stop being a little bitch. He actually called me a little bitch!"

"God, what an asshole!" I said.

"I tried another tactic, and I began to cry. I pleaded with him to take me home, but that only seemed to make him more determined, because he started driving even faster. So I stopped crying and tried threatening him. I told him that if he did anything to me, my dad would have him killed."

"What did he say to that?"

"He said, 'You're not going to tell your dad anything.' By then we were way up there at the top of the canyon, miles away. That's when he finally stopped the car. He pulled in to this parking spot, like a lover's lane or something, and unbuckled his seat belt. Then he said, 'Come on Wendy, enjoy the view.' Like we were on a real date or something."

"What a jerk."

"Before I could do anything, he unsnapped my seat belt and reached over and pushed me back against the car door. He already had both hands on my breasts. He didn't even bother trying to kiss me. He just started mashing my breasts and pushing me back against the door. I was trying to push him away with one hand and trying to get my other hand behind me to open the door, but he had me pinned against it. The next thing I knew, he grabbed the top of my dress and pulled it down, and it just ripped apart." Wendy looked down at her torn dress again. "It's silk. Then he grabbed the front of my bra and yanked it so hard it broke and came away in his hands. I think he hurt me when he did that. Can you take a look at my back? It feels like he cut me when he ripped off my bra."

I unzipped the back of what was left of Wendy's dress. Sure enough, there were welts on her back where her bra had cut into her and a small gash, probably from the clasp. "Yes, you're pretty bruised, and there's a cut too. We should probably get you cleaned up. You can use my shower, and then we can put some ointment on your cuts and get some arnica on those bruises."

"Thank you, Lucy," she said, gratefully. She leaned back against the sofa again, still trying to cover her chest with her torn dress.

"But how did you manage to get away?" I asked.

"He finally started to kiss me, shoving his tongue down my throat, making me gag. At the same time, he pulled my skirt up so he could get his hand between my legs. He managed to get as far as my panties when I suddenly realized he was in the perfect position for me to get my knee up into his groin. That's when I kneed him with all my might. You should have heard him scream! He actually screamed!"

"Fantastic," I said.

"Then, I grabbed my purse and jumped out of the car before he could get his senses back. I shouted, 'Die, you motherfucker!' like I was in a Tarantino movie or something. I took my shoes off right away so I could run, and I ran like my life depended on it. All the way down that hill, all the way back here. Oh God, my feet are killing me!"

"Did he try to go after you?"

"I don't think so. But I couldn't be sure. I hid in the bushes if I heard a car coming, and his little Lotus is pretty loud. I would have recognized it. I think he just gave up and drove home."

"I can't believe you walked all the way here. Why didn't you phone a taxi or something?"

"I don't know. I wasn't thinking. And anyway, I don't know any taxi numbers. I was just so afraid someone would see me and somehow my dad would find out. I can't let him know. You won't tell anyone, will you?"

"Of course not."

"I'm just so glad you were up. I was afraid to go home. Can I stay here for a while?"

"Yes, of course," I said. I stood up and took Wendy's hand and pulled her up from the sofa. "Let's get you in the shower now. Look, your knees are all skinned too."

"Oh yeah. I fell down a couple of times while I was running away."

"You poor thing."

I put Wendy in my shower. Fortunately, I had an en-suite bathroom, which was very cool for a teenager. It had a tub and shower. While Wendy let the water wash away her terror, I scrubbed her back as gently as I could.

Wendy had a wonderful dancer's body, all muscle and toned skin, with powerful legs and firm buttocks. Her breasts were small and round, like dancer's breasts often were, with the tiniest pink nipples right in the center of each one. She had a soft, round face, totally at odds with her slim, toned body.

Her mouth was small, and her lips were thin, but she had good teeth, like most kids in West LA, but her nose was kind of shapeless, not big enough to warrant a nose job, but not small enough to be cute. Her eyes were very blue, and when they weren't swollen from crying, they were her most attractive feature. When she was made up and especially when she was dancing, she could look fabulous. She wasn't my type physically, and while I was scrubbing her wounded back, I tried not to sexualize her. I knew she was in a vulnerable state. She'd been totally traumatized by her near rape.

After her shower, we put antiseptic and Band-Aids on all her wounds. Then I gave her some of my clothes to wear, just jeans and a sweatshirt. It was pretty late, so we walked down the hill to her house and snuck her through the screen on her back window, which fortunately was open a crack, so we could push it open the rest of the way easily. Jonny had been right about one thing: she would never tell her parents what had happened.

We crumpled up her torn dress and wrapped it in a grocery bag and threw it in a dumpster on the way to school the next day.

But then an amazing thing happened to Jonny. Just before the summer break, Jonny was on his way back to his home on Bellagio Road after one of his so-called dates. It was after midnight when he suddenly lost control of his precious Lotus and spun it off one of those high, sweeping curves on Bellagio. He crashed into the canyon below, and his car caught on fire. He managed to survive, but with more than 60 percent burns over his body *and* his face, as well as a lot of internal injuries. When he regained consciousness in the burn unit at the USC Hospital, he was raving about seeing Carmen in his rearview mirror just as he came into that turn. He claimed she was sitting in the backseat of his car, smiling her wicked smile.

I believed him.

CHAPTER 9
SUMMERTIME BLUES

I WAS still deep in the throes of pain and misery when school let out for the summer. I hadn't really done anything but study since Carmen's murder, so my grades were fantastic, but my heart was sick. I hadn't been able to continue my tutoring of Wendy because I couldn't bring myself to walk down there, and the thought of dancing made me nauseous. I did continue to visit Angela and James, as James had taken the semester off to be with his mom.

Oddly, since Carmen's death, Angela had stopped drinking. Just like that. She was sober all the time now, so she was gracefully somber instead of charmingly loopy. The toothpaste advert smile was completely gone now, and she no longer looked like the mom from *Leave It to Beaver*, but she was still ever so sweet and hospitable. On an invitation from my mom, Angela had taken up bridge and was now part of a foursome playing cards with my mom every Thursday night and hosting a bridge luncheon every Sunday afternoon.

Even with all that, it was still pretty grim across the street. Neither of them could bring themselves to do anything with Carmen's room. All they had managed so far was to shut the door. They hadn't made any attempt to pack anything up and never bothered to lock it, so sometimes when I was over there and feeling particularly sorry for myself, I would go into Carmen's room and lie on her bed and cry.

I began hanging out with James more and more, particularly on the weekends. He was living there like an adult son, mostly reading and studying for the exams he would be facing when he returned to the academy in the fall. He and I gradually started feeling less self-conscious with each other, and often we simply watched TV together over at his house or slipped off to Pip's for cheesecake and coffee.

That was where I finally decided to ask him about the little black dress.

"Carmen never told you about the dress?" He seemed genuinely surprised.

"No," I answered. "And the one time I asked, she almost bit my head off, and I thought she would hate me forever."

"Well. I can't really explain this psychologically," he continued, "but I can give you a little bit of history about it, which might help. In fact, I think it was the history of that dress that made it irresistible for her. I think she felt compelled to wear it."

"What are you talking about?" I asked, more mystified than ever.

"I'm surprised that my mother didn't tell you about it either. You would think she would have made some attempt to explain." And he looked down at his slice of cheesecake and picked up his fork. Then he paused for a moment. "Of course, my mom was drinking quite a bit then. Maybe she didn't even notice." He took a bite, savoring it for a second with his eyes closed, and then he opened them and looked across at me, his blue eyes shining. "That was the dress my mom wore to my dad's funeral."

"You're kidding!" I exclaimed, absolutely stunned. "The *exact* same dress?"

"Yup. After the funeral, Carmen just swiped it from my mom's bedroom, hemmed it up that very night, and started wearing it the next day."

"Wow," I exclaimed, digesting this tidbit. "Didn't you think that was a bit strange?"

"Well, of course I did. But I didn't know what to make of it, and I didn't want to make a big deal of it either. The whole business of my dad dying had been pretty shocking, and I didn't want to say anything that would open any more wounds. So I just pretended not to notice. At first I thought, well, it's a pretty dress, and she looks great in it, so what's the harm? But then, when she started wearing it every single day, I thought, well, this is weird, but I still didn't know what to do about it—and like you, I didn't dare ask."

"Okay, so she starts wearing her mom's funeral dress," I said after a while. "I think that explains a lot, but not everything. I am going to need a bit more information. There has to be a solid reason behind it somewhere."

"Well, she had been pretty angry with my mother for staying with my dad after I left. So I knew that was an issue they hadn't resolved. The more I think about it, the more I begin to think it was her way of always reminding my mother of his existence—like the elephant in the room— because my mother had allowed our father to exist in our house. Carmen hated him. You do know that, don't you? And rightly so. I think she probably couldn't forgive mom for staying with him, but because she loved our mother, she couldn't do anything to really hurt her. I think she just kept wearing the dress to hurt her without *deliberately* hurting her.... Does that make any sense?"

"Yes. That makes a weird kind of sense. I can see that. And maybe she wanted to keep reminding herself that her dad was really dead?" I offered.

"Right. I never thought of that. But that's good. You should be a psychologist!"

"My mom's one, remember?" In truth, I had read a lot of the psychology books my mom kept in her office library, but that didn't make me an expert. It did help me understand that no one could know exactly how another mind really worked, and it did give me a few insights into *why* our minds work the way they do.

"And," I continued, "I think she must have considered it some form of armor to shield herself from the past, or maybe just for keeping other guys at a distance? What do you think?"

"That's a good point too," he said, and then he put his head in his hands and said one more thing. "If only it could have worked that way."

I didn't want to start crying in Pips, so I pretended to rearrange the sugar packets and changed the subject.

"My parents are taking me away this summer."

"Oh really?" James asked, brightening up a bit. "Where are they taking you?"

"They're taking the family on 'The Grand Tour': England, France, Switzerland, Italy, and Spain. It's an expensive remedy that my mom cooked up to make me forget this year. My little brother gets to come on my dime. But that's okay too."

"That's great! I think it will be fantastic. You'll see all kinds of fabulous things, and you'll love it."

"Yup. And I get to share the experience with my parents and my little brother. Whoop-de-do!"

"Seriously, you'll be glad you went—and you will have something else besides calculus to occupy your mind."

But calculus and every other course I studied was just mental gymnastics to me. They didn't occupy my mind at all. They took up only one little corner of it. The rest was filled with Carmen. There wasn't room for anything or anyone else.

CHAPTER 10
MY SUMMER VACATION

WE WERE on the plane to Heathrow the day after school broke for the summer. Brand-new passports, brand-new luggage, same old heartache. The entire time I kept wishing Carmen could have been there with me. I had become so used to sharing every experience with her, and there were so many times I wanted to say, "Hey, look at that!" or "Did you read this?" or whatever, just wanting to share all the new things with her the way we used to.

Record stores were the worst. I kept finding these really neat specialty shops in all these amazing cities we visited throughout England and Europe, full of all kinds of interesting EPs and vinyl. But now I stalked the record stores and prowled the bookstores alone, with no one to share my discoveries while my indulgent parents and bored little brother waited for me in the local cafés. Don't get me wrong, it was still a lovely experience, and there were at least a few minutes out of every day when I did not think about Carmen, but oh, if she had only been there with me....

It was when we arrived in Italy, halfway through our trip, that I began to experience the nightmares for the first time. Although they weren't exactly nightmares—more like nighttime visions. I don't know if it was because there were so many gorgeous dark-haired girls in Italy who resembled Carmen or what, but the visions began there and stayed with me for the remainder of the trip. Even my nightly Valium couldn't make them go away.

They came on almost as soon as I shut my eyes and let myself fall into that first layer of sleep. Suddenly, there was Carmen. But this time she would be standing by her own graveside, her mourners all around her. She would be standing silently at the very edge of her own grave, staring straight at me with an expression so baleful and forlorn, it could break anyone's heart.

Even in the daylight, I couldn't shake the memory of that dream, that desolate look in her eyes. I couldn't shake the feeling she was trying to communicate with me, that she was imploring me to do something. That was when I knew I had to find her killers. She would never rest until I did.

CHAPTER 11
HOME AGAIN

MY FAMILY made it back to LA with everyone in one piece, except for me. I was *still* in pieces. Carmen hadn't given me much rest on this vacation, and now I needed to find out if there had been any progress in the investigation into her murder while I'd been away. Just as soon as I rebounded from my jetlag, I went across the street to see how Carmen's family was doing. James answered the door, and I was so happy to see he was still staying there, I gave him a great big hug. Angela was right behind him, and I gave her a big hug too. I guess I had missed them more than I realized.

With their usual Southern politeness, they wanted to know all about my European adventures, but all I wanted was to be updated on the police investigation.

"They've still got nothing," James told me. "They've been back over here at least three times during the summer, asking the same questions. They still seem to think Carmen went willingly with those creeps."

"Crap" was all I could say. "So there's nothing new at all? When I left, they seemed to be checking out similar crimes in the state. They didn't come up with anything?"

"No. Nothing."

Angela had gone off to the kitchen to fetch some iced tea. I wanted to change the subject, so I asked James how his mom was doing.

"Actually, she seems a lot better," he answered. "I think she's going to recover. But it's so weird now that she isn't drinking. We can have real conversations again, and we watch TV together most nights without her nodding off." He actually smiled then.

"That's great to hear. So what about you? How are *you* doing?"

"Well, I'm ready to go back to the academy. I think Mom's going to be okay now, but it would make me feel a lot better if I knew you would keep stopping by now and then."

"No problem, of course I will. I can call you on your cell if there's any news. I'll keep you updated as much as I can."

"So," he said, and paused before going on. "How are *you* doing, Carmen-wise? Is it getting any better?"

"Well, I'm still taking Valium to get to sleep, but I'm not crying so much in the daytime anymore. And I think I can manage this last year of school. I've already been accepted to Santa Cruz, so I don't have to worry too much about schoolwork anymore."

"I thought you were planning to go back east for college, Columbia or something?"

"I was. But that was then. Now I don't feel comfortable leaving the state until they catch Carmen's killers. I just don't feel like I can move that far away from here yet." Meaning I didn't feel comfortable leaving Carmen.

"Wow. What do your folks think about that?"

"Actually, my mom's delighted. She's happy to have me closer to home. My dad's not too keen, but he's still reeling from the disappointment that, with all my brains, I didn't follow him into medicine. So they'll adjust no matter what, and I can transfer wherever I like later. Right now, I just don't know what I'm doing. I'm just going to coast along until my brain relaxes."

Angela came back with the iced tea, and we sat around and made small talk about the benefits of world travel for the rest of the afternoon.

When I got back to my house, I called Wendy to tell her I was home. She came over later, and we went over our school schedules together. My senior year was about to start, but without any of the excitement I had expected when I entered high school as a freshman. I was resigned to facing my life the way it was going to be now, but I couldn't get enthusiastic about it.

Wendy was no substitute for Carmen, but we had been friends since the seventh grade, when my dad had our house built on the corner of her street, and my family moved here from Brentwood. Now, after all that had happened this past year, it made sense to get closer to her again. We didn't have much in common, but we'd always had a sort of symbiotic relationship. I helped her with her schoolwork, and she helped me navigate the intricate social life of the West LA teen scene.

The truth was, I had been a complete nerd up until I turned fifteen. Until then, I had been a little redheaded bookworm with lots of freckles and no sense of style. As I grew older, I only seemed to get more introverted, and then, two monumental things happened: first, I found out I was gay. And next, I discovered my mom's ancient CD collection. It was full of eighties morbid-sounding music and the stuff they used to call "shoegazer" music. I began listening to bands like The Cure, The Smiths, and the Cocteau Twins. My iPod was full of music no one else would be caught dead listening to.

Then, somehow, during the summer before my fifteenth birthday, I grew four inches taller, and my body started taking on something close to an actual shape. My face began to rearrange itself in a surprising but not unpleasant way. My freckles faded, and my cheekbones became more prominent, while my eyes, which had always seemed small and colorless to me, suddenly turned out to be an amazing shade of green and weren't so small after all. By the time the school year came around, I looked kind of cute.

My new cuteness wouldn't help my position on the popularity scales in high school. It was too late for that. Once a nerd, always a nerd, and I had been branded one way back in junior high when Bobby Zuckerman asked me to dance at one of those junior Saturday-night dances. He totally threw me off-balance when he pulled me close to him for a slow dance. He pulled me so close I could feel every part of his body, and I didn't like what I felt! I yelled, "Get off me!" and pushed him away and went running to the girls' room.

Everybody heard me, and I was too embarrassed to come out of the girls' room until Wendy finally managed to sneak me out through a side door during a fast dance when nobody was looking. But the damage was done. Bobby ran with the elite crowd, and I had just demonstrated in front of the entire junior high school student body what an immature little nerd I truly was. I was just lucky I had Wendy to keep the bullies off me afterward.

Along with my interest in weird music, I finally began to develop a degree of individuality and style. Over the next year, Wendy did a bit of a makeover on me too. She lightened my hair with this easy-to-use rinse, so I became a strawberry blonde instead of a scary redhead. Then she taught me how to wear makeup and took me shopping to further hone my "style" so that I learned what looked good on me and enhanced my natural attributes without compromising my dark sensibilities and my desire to remain unconventional.

So by the time Carmen came into my life, I was a five-foot-four strawberry blonde with a fine little face, good teeth, and green eyes. My outfit of choice was tight black jeans and a long, deep crimson or purple-colored top with lots of belts and scarves. I wore my hair long, with big hoop earrings that suited me best. Oh yes, Wendy was responsible for that too; she pierced my ears for me with a sewing needle.

So even though I kept putting her down, she had always been a good friend to me, and with her dad being this big-shot Hollywood blockbuster director, she could walk among the top cliques at our school. Her friendship had always afforded me protection from the usual torments. And to her credit, she only grazed among that crowd without ever actually belonging to it. Her heart was totally devoted to dancing, and when she was not at school, she was working out with her personal choreographer. She didn't have time for petty school politics because she was absolutely driven. I felt I was lucky she still wanted to be my friend after all the time I spent ignoring her.

We passed the weekend after my return from Europe preparing ourselves for the new semester. I showed her my prospectus for Santa Cruz, and she showed me her acceptance letter from the American Musical and Dramatic Academy in New York, known as the AMDA.

"That's fantastic. I heard it was really impossible to get into that school unless you're totally talented!" I exclaimed, giving her a big hug. "And you know you are."

"Yeah. They have these monster auditions, and you have to be recommended by your choreographers too," she said, kind of dismissively. "But my dad is furious with me. He said it's not a real university, and I should stay out of show business anyway. He really hates it."

"God, I was hoping he'd got over that by now."

"Nope, he's just dead set against it, but he can't stop me," she said, "I love it too much, and I'm damned good at it. I'm a lot better dancer than I'll ever be a student."

"Well, he *will* get over it," I assured her. "He's probably trying to protect you from an industry he knows is pretty corrupt and cruel."

Sunday afternoon, James called me to say his cab was coming to take him to the airport, and I ran over, and we said our tearful good-byes. I stayed late with Angela, and we made a batch of brownies to drown our sorrow in. Then I went home to take a look at my choice of outfits for the next day. Classes were beginning on Monday.

Time was just going to keep right on going, and I had to get on with the rest of my life. The rest of my new life, that is, the one without Carmen.

CHAPTER 12
THE NEW BOY

ASIDE FROM haunting my dreams, I didn't know what Carmen's ghost got up to over the summer. All I knew was that the rumors started up again as soon as the semester began.

I still didn't know if it was simple hysteria on the part of the male student body brought on by the rumors of Carmen's ghost or what, but now *all* the new kids seemed to be experiencing these same hallucinations or visitations or whatever. I never could explain it adequately because I never experienced any of these visitations myself, but after a while, I simply took it upon myself to protect Carmen's memory as well as the mental health of these new kids, and I began to look out for any new male arrivals.

I wanted to get ahold of them before they were contaminated by the stories circulating throughout our campus. I took to patrolling the hallways, as unobtrusively as possible. Sometimes, I actually volunteered for hall patrol, which was a duty seniors could take on during their free periods but was usually the purview of the most craven Goody Two-shoes. It mainly meant you were supposed to bust kids who were skipping class or smoking on campus. I didn't like pretending I gave a shit about school rules, but I wanted a chance to explain this phenomenon to any new kid I spotted and give him my spin on the ghost stories so that they made some sense.

So when I saw this tall skinny kid leaning against the wall outside the door to the chem lab, his face drained of all color, staring down the hall with his mouth open, I could tell right away he was the new boy in school.

He had obviously lost his way. No one else was around because class had already started, and he was alone in the corridor. I walked right up to him in a casual, nonthreatening way so as not to frighten him any further, and said, "You look like you've seen a ghost."

He stared down at me, eyeing me carefully to make certain I was real before answering, "I think I just did!"

I leaned back against the wall beside him. "Yup, you probably did," I agreed. "Tell me what you saw."

I looked him over while he answered. He wasn't a bad-looking guy, but the poor thing had that geeky look boys his age get when they are late bloomers. Those are the kinds of boys who have their massive growth spurt late in their teens, around about seventeen, becoming suddenly and unexpectedly miles taller, and therefore, unused to their new height, they become terribly awkward and clumsy, bumping into things and knocking things over while their faces grow bonier and their bodies become leaner because they can't keep enough food in themselves to compensate for all this new growth.

"I was late to class," he began. "I couldn't find the chemistry lab, and all of a sudden, the bell rang, and I was the only one in the halls. I heard this sound, this tapping sound, like high-heeled shoes walking behind me, like they were following me, maybe teasing me. So I turned around, and there was no one there!" He looked at me to see if I believed him, and I just nodded and let him go on.

"I decided to walk back down that hallway and see if somebody was playing a joke or something, but as soon as I started walking in the other direction, I began to hear those footsteps again, but behind me now, just tap, tap, tapping like a woman in high heels walking right behind me. I turned around real fast, but there was no one there again, except this time I thought I caught a glimpse of someone stepping around the next corner, a girl in a black dress. I don't know, but I blinked my eyes for a second and she was gone." And he shook his head in disbelief and looked hard at me. "You are real, aren't you?"

"Oh yes, I am certainly real," I assured him. "But listen, I'm kind of your, um, unofficial guide, and I need to explain a little about what you just heard and maybe saw. You need to come with me now."

He was staring at me again like I might be crazy, but I just went on, "Look, I'm real, and I know some things that will help you, so just let's get out of this hallway, okay?" He still looked doubtful, but I kept talking. "It's your first day, right? You can skip this class. Everything is always chaotic on a kid's first day. The administration won't care, and your teachers won't care either. Come with me; we need to talk."

Luckily, he was still so obviously awestruck that he let me lead him down the hall to the seniors' lounge, where I had special privileges on account of my grade point average and my association with Carmen. The seniors' lounge is very cool; it's tucked away in the arts workshop part of the school, so the lower grades don't come near it, and it provides a respite for those seniors with good grades. We can use it for study or for a place to hang out in during our free periods. It's equipped with sofas, study tables, and computers, as well as a coffee machine and a couple of vending machines with sandwiches and snacks.

"Hey, this is cool. Are you sure we're really allowed in here?"

"This is the senior lounge. You *are* a senior, aren't you?"

"Yes," he said, putting his book bag down on one of the tables.

"How about a coffee?"

"We're allowed coffee at school?"

"You're a senior, remember? This is one of the approved drugs for seniors. Milk and sugar?" I asked, and he nodded, as I expected he would, and I brewed two cups of slightly chemical-tasting coffee in the handy brewing machine, and we sat down at one of the tables.

"I'm Lucy, by the way."

"I'm Seth Greenberg," he offered with a toothy smile, revealing the appropriate amount of orthodontia necessary for life in LA.

"Where did you transfer from?" I asked, always curious.

"We're from Austin, Texas."

"Wow!" I exclaimed, genuinely impressed. "How did you get here, of all places?" We didn't get very many Texans in LA.

"My dad's a police detective, a captain, actually, homicide. He just got this offer from the LAPD and took it. He's kind of a specialist in his field, one of the new-style 'homicide criminologists' with a PhD. They've got him working on the latest unsolved murders already, and we've only been in town for three days!"

Oh my God! I thought. *How perfect is this? He can help me. He has to have been sent here to help me find Carmen's killers!*

I told Seth the whole gruesome story about Carmen's murder and my association with her. I made sure he understood how truly awful it was those creeps were still at large and still out there somewhere. I wanted him to understand how important this was, and most of all, I wanted to make sure he talked to his father about it.

"Christ! That's awful," he exclaimed, and he seemed honestly appalled by my story. "We've got to do something about this. That's just horrible. I'll help in whatever way I can." Just like that. He sincerely wanted to help.

We spent the next half hour talking about what he could do to get his father interested in the case or at least find out if his father was already working on it, and if so, how far he had gotten.

I wasn't looking for a new best friend right then; I was simply floating on the hope of finding Carmen's killers at last. But then I asked Seth where he was living.

"We're living in Brentwood right now. Just renting."

"That's pretty far from where I live," I remarked.

"I've got a car," he answered.

I didn't know then that, from that point on, I would be seeing Seth nearly every day, and in the next few weeks, I would tell Seth everything there was to know about Carmen and me.

CHAPTER 13
HOPE

SETH WAS waiting for me outside the front entrance after school that day. He was easy to spot, being so tall and skinny and dressed like a geek. He was probably the only boy in my school trying *not* to look cool. We walked together to the parking lot.

"I have no idea what happened in any of my classes today," he said. "All I could think about was your friend, Carmen. I can't get her murder out of my mind." He shuffled beside me through the throngs of normal LA high school kids, with their normal, angst-filled, privileged lives, hurrying to their flashy cars their folks had given them for their sixteenth birthdays. "I want to talk to my dad about it tonight."

"Gee," I said, looking down at the sidewalk, which was covered in little round circlets of dried gum. I didn't know what to say. I was too excited and hopeful. "Where's your car?" I asked.

"I didn't know where to park, so it's in the visitors' lot, right here, actually," and he pointed toward a little black Honda Civic, definitely not a prestigious car but reliable, parked close to the admin building.

"You're lucky you didn't get a ticket," I remarked.

"I asked for a visitor's permit," he said. Of course he had. He was a policeman's son. He'd do everything by the book, I thought. How wrong I was. "Where's yours?" he asked, opening the back door of his car and throwing his book bag on the backseat. "Want me to give you a ride to it?"

"Sure," I said, climbing into the passenger seat. "I'll show you where I park. It's the best place, really." He got in the car and put on his seat belt, and then we just looked at each other. I guess my face looked pretty grim, because he suddenly brightened up.

"I know my dad's going to help," he said. Seth's eyes were a gray-blue, like ice, but they were honest eyes, and I knew he meant what he said. "You'll see. He's going to find her killers. He can do it. He's really good at his job." He started the engine, and I directed him through the maze of parking lots to the student lot at the back of the theater arts building where I always parked. It had easy access to my homeroom, and there was always a space there because everyone else liked to park near the gym. I pointed out my little red car to Seth, and he pulled in beside it.

"This is amazing, Seth," I said, "I can't believe that your dad's a homicide detective. It's fantastic. But how are you going to talk to him? Won't your dad think you're meddling in police business?"

"I'll just tell him how I met you and how we got talking—"

"But you won't tell him that you thought you saw Carmen's ghost, right?" I interrupted.

"No, of course not. I'll definitely leave that part out. Maybe I'll just say I met you in the senior lounge."

"Right, and we just got to talking. That's normal, right?" I don't know why I was suddenly obsessed with appearing normal. Seth certainly didn't look normal. He was gangly and dressed like a geek. He was going to have a hard time fitting in as a senior here at Uni High. None of his clothes had designer labels on them, and he was wearing a short-sleeved plaid shirt, for God's sake, so that his skinny arms stuck out like the "before" picture in a muscle-drink advertisement.

"Look, don't worry, Lucy," he said, smiling a slightly crooked big-toothed smile. "I'll know what to say. I'll find out if my dad's already working on the case or not, and if he's not, I'll tell him all about you and see if I can get him to check into it."

"But not too much about me," I said.

"Just enough so he realizes how important this is."

"Thanks, Seth. Here, you better take my number in case you need to ask me anything." We exchanged texts so we had each other's numbers in our phones' contact list. Then I opened the door and leaned in to say good-bye.

"It was great meeting you," I said.

"Yeah, me too," he said. "I'm going to help, you'll see. Meet me here before class tomorrow? I may need you to show me how to get to homeroom." He smiled that crooked smile again. He didn't look too bad when he smiled, I decided.

"Sure, and maybe you can call me tonight if you have any news about Carmen?"

"I will," he said. I shut the door and waved a good-bye as he drove off to wherever he lived in Brentwood.

I climbed into my little Mazda and drove out of the school lot and through the streets of West LA without seeing a thing, my head buzzing with new possibilities. I don't even remember what route I took. All I know is when I got home, I surprised my brother by actually eating one of Constanza's abundant after-school snacks. I had an appetite for the first time since the day Carmen disappeared.

Seth telephoned me just after we finished our dinner, which, to my mother's great pleasure, I ate most of. It was a good thing he called, because I was so agitated I couldn't concentrate on anything at all.

As soon as I saw his name come up on my phone, I said a quick "hi" and ran down the stairs to my bedroom. I didn't want anyone listening in.

"I talked to my dad," Seth said.

"How did it go?" I asked, trying not to sound too hopeful.

"I just told him how I met you and how we started talking and how you were connected to this girl named Carmen that had been murdered last year."

"Wow," I said.

"My dad wasn't surprised that I knew about Carmen's murder. He already knew your name too."

"He did?"

"Yes. He seemed to know all about you, that's why he asked me how you were doing."

"What did you tell him?"

"I told him the truth. That you were depressed and disappointed and that you didn't think the police were looking hard enough to find her killers."

"What did your dad say?"

"He told me that he already knew all about the case and that it was a top priority. I kind of got the feeling that he thought the LAPD hadn't done such a good job on the investigation."

"Did he say that?"

"Not in so many words. He plays things close to the vest. But he told me he was planning to reinterview you this very week. In fact, he's going to reinterview everyone as soon as he can."

"That's amazing," I sighed, biting my own lip. I was afraid I was going to burst into tears at any moment.

"He also told me, in no uncertain terms, that he had no intention of sharing any information about the case with me. Period," Seth added.

"Oh gosh," I said, disappointed that I wouldn't have an inside into any information after all. "That's too bad."

"Oh, don't worry about that," Seth said, chuckling. "I'm a computer geek. I've been hacking into my dad's computer for years. If my dad isn't willing to share his information, I'll figure out another way of obtaining it."

"You can do that?"

"Yes, I can," he assured me. "We'll keep tabs on the investigation, don't worry. I better go now. I'll see you before class tomorrow."

"Okay," I said. "And, Seth, thanks so much for this. You don't know what it means to me."

"It's okay. I'm going to need your help to navigate around that school of yours. See you tomorrow."

After we hung up, I lay down on one of my beds and stared up at the soundproofing squares in the ceiling and thought about Carmen. They were going to find her killers at last. Knowing this didn't stop me from missing her terribly. It didn't stop the rage I felt when I thought about how her life had ended in such a horrible way. Or that we would never be able to talk together again, lying just like this on the two little beds in my room, staring up at the ceiling and listening to music together, or that we would never finish exploring our new sexual relationship, the relationship that had started out so tentatively, so shyly, because it was so new to both of us.

Mostly, we had only kissed and cuddled. I'd never kissed anyone before except this gay boy in drama class a few years ago. I had confessed to him that I'd never been kissed and that I was embarrassed because I didn't know how.

"I'll teach you," he offered.

And he did. Backstage, behind the scenery, waiting for our entrance, me dressed in my rabbit suit and him dressed in his bear outfit, we kissed. His lips were soft, and his mouth tasted clean and sweet.

"Just open your mouth a little," he said, "and don't freak out. I'm just going to slide my tongue between your lips."

It was weird, because it was totally nonsexual. It was like a tongue exercise, but I learned to open my mouth and let him slide his tongue between my teeth, and then I did the same to him, and we practiced that a few times, and that was it.

So when Carmen and I came home after that first day at Shakespeare's, we ran down to my room as usual, shut the door behind us, but this time I locked it. Carmen had walked to the back windows overlooking the patio and shut the drapes, making the room suddenly go dark. We met in the middle of the room, next to my desk, and that was where we had our first kiss. We just embraced like friends, and then I kissed her. I started it. It was as if Carmen, who was so ravishingly beautiful, had never been kissed before. But she opened her mouth when I pressed my lips against hers and kissed me back with a sudden frenzy as soon as she felt my tongue slide against hers.

The next thing I knew, we were lying on one of my single beds, our tongues and lips glued together and her little black dress was sliding up over her head and my hands were on her soft breasts and I was moaning and panting and grinding my hips against hers, and before we could go any further, I ground myself into an orgasm, shuddering against her mouth.

After that first experience, we went a lot further, but never all the way. Carmen never let me get between her thighs. She would let me caress her mound with the tips of my fingers, but that was as close as I could get. She had the most luscious tangle of black hair down there, making my thin, light-colored bush seem puny by comparison, and we shaved each other's into interesting shapes, but she never let me slip so much as a finger between the lips of her sex, let alone my tongue.

She happily went down on me, though, her wet tongue like a magical device that would make me come like the proverbial rocket, but she never let me return the favor. Most of the time we just kissed and cuddled. She liked to cuddle. She liked to cuddle and fall asleep in my arms. It was beautiful and comforting, and I loved how she felt lying beside me, so soft and womanly. But I always imagined someday she would let me make love to her the way she made love to me. I would take it slow. I loved her. I could wait. I never imagined she would be taken away from me before she could know what it was like to be made love to like that. I never imagined I would never even get to hold her in my arms again.

Chapter 14
The Interview

When I arrived at school the next morning, Seth's little Honda was already parked in my usual slot, so I pulled in alongside it. Seth was sitting in his car, reading his transfer notes and looking at a map of the school when I tapped on his window.

"Hey," he said after opening his window.

"Hey," I answered. "Did you figure out where your homeroom was?"

"Well, I was trying to do that just now. The homeroom teacher seems to be a Mr. Moskowitz. Do you know him?"

"That's great! He's my homeroom teacher too. Just come along with me. He's actually pretty cool. He's a secret mathematician, so you two will probably get along great."

We walked together to homeroom, chatting about schoolwork and the rest of Seth's teachers. He was in most of the same advanced placement classes I was, but all his electives were in math while mine were in theater and art. We parted after the homeroom roll call. He had to undergo some more indoctrination, and I had to get to art history. We arranged to meet during the first break. We were already friends. It was pretty effortless and had nothing to do with any of that boyfriend/girlfriend bullshit. In fact, it was precisely because neither of us seemed to feel any of that "mating pair" peer pressure that we were able to slide into each other's lives so easily.

Seth's dad telephoned me on my cell during lunch to make an appointment with me.

"Hello," he said. "Is this Lucy Linsky?" He had a pleasantly masculine voice with a soft Texas twang. "This is Captain Greenberg of LAPD Homicide Division. I'd like to meet you and go over some details having to do with your friend's murder."

"Sure," I said, hiding my anxiety behind small words. "When?"

"I'd like to come to your house as soon as possible. Your mother needs to be present, so you may want to talk to her first."

"Oh, it's all right. She'll be happy to be there whenever it's convenient for you," I said, and I wasn't lying. My mom had been present for all the other police interviews, and I knew she would be happy to shift her own appointments around so she could meet the new captain of the LAPD Homicide Division.

"Tomorrow at 4:00 p.m.? Would that be a good time? Will you be home from school by then?"

"Yes, that's great. I'll let my mom know." I gave him my address again and hung up.

I was in a state of high anxiety from that moment on, and the school day seemed to last forever. It was useless for me to be there, but the next day was even worse. I went to school anyway, just to see Seth. Fortunately, I had two free periods after lunch, so I hung out in the seniors' lounge and plotted and planned and imagined what I was going to say to Seth's father, Captain Greenberg.

Then Wendy came in for her free period and kept me entertained with some interesting news about the cheerleading squad. Usually, I smiled and zoned out during Wendy's chatter, but today her conversation was curiously dark, and I listened and took a lot of mental notes. Although Wendy wasn't exactly popular, she was blonde and athletic and knew how to be friendly to the right people. The right people, in this case, were the cheerleading squad.

"Something definitely weird is going on in the cheerleading squad," she announced, sitting down and opening a peach yogurt. *Who cares?* was my immediate reaction, but I didn't say it out loud. I just looked up with a big question mark on my face, because I knew Wendy was going to tell me no matter what.

"I mean it," she said, leaning forward and looking at me with an unusually serious expression on her plump little face. "I know you don't like the cheerleaders, and you don't care, but I've got a few friends on the squad, and they're worried about something."

"Yes, well, they should be worried about devoting themselves to such a ridiculous endeavor," I answered, rather meanly.

Wendy dropped a spoonful of yogurt into her mouth and ignored my comment. "Have you heard about all the injuries they're having this year?"

"I don't really pay any attention to anything about cheerleading."

"Well, my friend Andrea showed up at school yesterday with her arm in a sling. She claims she dislocated her shoulder learning the new routines. In fact, *all* the girls are complaining about the new routines, but I think there's more to it than that."

She sat back and looked at me, her blonde eyebrows raised, waving her spoon in the air like a magic wand.

"What do you mean?" I asked to be polite.

"I think that's just an excuse. They have new routines every year. They're supposed to have them, but this year, something is different. They all seem so down somehow, I mean the squad," she said. "I think there is something else going on, and they're blaming the routines instead of talking about it."

"What do you mean?"

"These injuries, for one thing. It's not just Andrea. Last week, Natalie came to school with a black eye. She said she had earned it when one of the other girls accidently elbowed her in the eye during a routine."

"Every year there are some minor injuries on the squad, even I know that," I said.

"No, it's different this year. Either the girls are becoming unusually accident prone or something really strange is going on. I just know something has changed, and it isn't just the routines."

"What do you mean?"

"I can't explain it, but I'm worried about my friend Caroline. She only just made the squad for the first time this year. She was over the moon when she made the final cut, but now she's all depressed. She told me last week that she thought she really wasn't cut out for it after all, and maybe she should quit."

"Well, that's probably a good thing. Shows she's growing up," I said.

"No, believe me, it's not a good thing. The whole squad seems depressed, like they've lost their usual spark."

"Well, I guess that can't be a good thing for a cheerleading squad."

Wendy shook her head and got up, throwing her yogurt cup into the recycling bin. "Well, bye, then. Off to fail another algebra quiz."

After Wendy slipped away to her algebra class, I tucked those tidbits she'd told me away to mull over later, and then Seth popped in, reminding me we had a world history class together.

"Great. This is my last class, and then I get to escape. I promise to tell you everything about the interview after your dad leaves."

Seth just chuckled. "I already figured out the passwords to my dad's files, and I bet I can get you the transcript of your own interview by tomorrow morning!"

Amazing, I thought to myself as I sat down at my desk.

I actually managed to sit still for the full hour, but I was out of my seat as soon as the bell rang.

"Talk to you later," I called as I ran down the hall.

Seth's dad arrived at our house at five minutes past four. I had been on the lookout for his car ever since I arrived home, and I had the door open as soon as he extricated his rather long body from the unmarked police car. He had somebody with him who was carrying a big brown leather briefcase.

"Hi," I said, holding open the door so they could walk past me into our foyer.

"Lucy Linsky, I believe?" Seth's father said, turning to face me. He was just as tall as I had expected, about six foot two, with the same dark hair and gray-blue eyes Seth had. He was handsome, though, as unlike Seth, his face had settled into an attractive maturity. Poor Seth needed a few more years before his face settled that way. Like Seth, he had a fine aquiline nose and a nice big mouth. The lines on his face indicated that he smiled a lot, and he smiled down at me as he introduced me to his partner. "This is Lieutenant Harrison, from the Robbery Homicide Special Case Division."

"Hello," I said, suddenly shy. Lieutenant Harrison was a very fit-looking young man, with light brown hair and serious brown eyes. He seemed to be studying our wallpaper, an exotic design of cranes and birds of paradise. "Uh, well, we thought it would be a good idea to meet in our kitchen. It's more comfortable there, and our housekeeper has made us some coffee and cookies, if you like."

I led them into the kitchen. Constanza had already made herself scarce, but she had left a fresh pot of coffee and a batch of her special cookies waiting for us on the counter. I yelled down the hall for my mom, who was in her study on the other side of the house. It was my mom who had decided we should use the kitchen instead of the den, because she knew they would be taping the interview, and it made sense to sit around a table.

It was a good thing too, because it turned out the briefcase the Lieutenant was carrying was full of all the old case files, and he took these out and laid them in piles in front of Captain Greenberg so they could refer to them. Then he set up the tape recorder.

After the first pleasantries were over and I had found out Seth's dad's first name was Michael and the lieutenant's name was Stan, we sat down with our coffee and cookies, and the lieutenant clicked on the recorder, made the usual announcement with the date and time, occupants of the room, etc., and we began.

I was impressed. Seth's dad was much more thorough than the other detectives had been. "All right, Lucy," he began, looking calmly at me with his ice-colored eyes. "In your previous statements, you say that Carmen didn't have a boyfriend and wasn't dating anyone at the time of her murder, is that right?"

"Yes, that's right," I answered. "She wasn't dating anyone ever. She wasn't interested in dating. She just wanted to get good grades, get into Columbia, and become a famous writer." As much as I wanted to tell him the truth, that Carmen and I were lovers and that she wouldn't think of dating anyone else but me, I wasn't ready to share that information with the outside world. I just hoped my word on the subject of dating would be convincing enough.

"You also said that several of the boys in your high school were coming on to her, and that some of them were quite persistent. Can you remember who any of these boys were?"

I laughed. "Aside from the entire male student body, you mean?"

"Yes, I mean were there any boys in particular that you could name," he prompted.

"Well, yes. There were several jocks that kept hitting on her and didn't seem to want to take no for an answer."

He handed me a pad and pencil. "Do you mind writing down their names?"

"No," I said, "I'll be happy to." And I began to list them. I tried to put them in descending order according to their level of persistence. Then I handed the list back to the captain, who gave it a quick glance before giving it to the lieutenant, who slid it into a new folder.

"If you think of anyone else, just e-mail me at the station. My e-mail address is on my card." He took a business card out of his pocket and handed it to me. It looked very official, stamped with the LAPD logo, and had his direct line and his e-mail address on it. I slipped it into my bra for safekeeping when he looked back down at his notes.

"Do you happen to know if any of these boys drive SUVs?"

"The school parking lot is full of them," I told him. "Practically every boy over sixteen drives some kind of sporty SUV nowadays. Most of them cost more than a home in The Valley. But I haven't paid any attention to who drives what car. I'm sorry."

"That's okay, Lucy, we can check it out from the school files." Then he asked me that same question all the cops had asked me before. "Do you think your friend Carmen would have willingly taken a lift from anyone she knew from school that day?"

"Absolutely not!" I said. "Not only would she not have given any of those jocks the time of day, but we were meeting up just down the street. It was a ten-minute walk. She didn't need a lift, and she didn't want a lift. She told me she wanted to walk."

"Do you usually meet up at that phone booth?" he asked, jotting down something in his notepad.

"Yes, we do" I said, sorry for my previous outburst. "It's convenient after I'd finished tutoring Wendy. I can just scoot down to the corner and pick up Carmen, and off we go. Wendy lives closer to that corner, and on sunny days, Carmen likes to sit out there on the guardrail and listen to the traffic." He looked at me oddly at that statement, but it was true. What else could I tell him?

"Do you think that Carmen might have been the kind of person to walk up to a vehicle if she knew the occupants? Let's say, if they drove by and stopped, and maybe rolled down their window to ask her a question?"

I nodded and began to feel sick to my stomach. "Yes, she would," I answered. "She was very polite, even when she was putting someone down."

"So she could have come close enough to a vehicle to be grabbed," he said solemnly. I nodded again. I couldn't say anything because all I could think about was my beautiful Carmen, the breeze blowing her hair, walking up to an ugly SUV, smiling her lovely smile just to be polite, and those creeps grabbing her and shoving her into the back of their car.

"Would you like some more coffee?" my mother asked, suddenly aware that I was losing it. I had forgotten she was even in the room. She hadn't sat down at the table. She had been leaning back against the sink and observing us, the way she does.

"Yes, please," I said.

"I might as well give you all a refill," she said, walking over with the coffee pot, looking cheerful and attractive for an older woman.

While I got myself together, pretending to examine the cookie plate, Captain Greenberg shuffled through the folders on the table. Then he looked over at me again and must have decided I was okay, because he began to ask me a totally different line of questions.

"You said in your statement that neither of you girls ever dated, but that you went out on the weekends to this place called the Sugar Shack. What is that, exactly?"

I explained that the Sugar Shack was a club almost exclusively frequented by girls and that we all just danced with each other.

"No one ever tried to hit on Carmen there?"

"The girls certainly didn't," I said, "and the few boys who hang out at the Sugar Shack are just nerdy muso types who know the DJs. Sometimes they watch us dance, but mainly they hang out by the turntable and talk about music with each other."

"And you don't think anyone showed a particular interest in Carmen?"

"Not that I noticed. Really. The girls just go there for the exercise and the music. Nobody goes there to pick up guys."

"This other club you went to, Shakespeare's? You said before that you were planning to go there on the day Carmen was abducted. That Carmen was going to do a reading?"

"Yes, it was poetry night."

"So this is some kind of coffee house? Some kind of alternative hangout?" he asked.

"Exactly," I told him. "We liked to go there because it was so cool and unusual. Most of the kids who go there are under eighteen, but there are some college kids too. Shakespeare's doesn't serve alcohol, though, so not too many older kids hang out there."

"And the clientele was mainly gay?" he asked, looking at me oddly again.

"Well, what I meant was that it was the kind of place where you could be yourself, whether you were gay or just hopelessly nerdy like me." That comment made the lieutenant smile. "A lot of arty kinds of kids hung out there, musicians and poets and maybe some of them are gay. That's all."

"I see," he said. "Did you happen to notice anyone paying particular attention to Carmen?"

"Never. We knew the owners and most of the regulars. Everybody there is friendly and supportive, like about our writing and stuff, but no one was stalking us or anything."

"Did you notice any SUVs or off-road vehicles parked in their parking lot?"

"No. I mean, there's a popular guitar store upstairs, so the parking lot is always full of cars. I never paid any attention to them. I was only happy to find a space for myself to park."

"Okay, then, Lucy. We're almost done here." He put down the pile of papers he was scanning and looked at me with his surprisingly gentle eyes. "I'm sorry, but I've got to ask you again about that ten minutes between the time Carmen called you on your cell phone and the time you drove to the phone booth and found she wasn't there."

I grimaced. There were those damned ten minutes again. If only it had been five minutes, and I had driven down there five minutes earlier. Would Carmen still be alive?

"Is it possible that she never even made it down to the phone booth at all?" he asked. "Could someone have picked her up outside her own house?"

"I don't know," I answered. "Do you?"

Captain Greenberg surprised me by actually answering. "I think it is entirely possible that she could have been picked up anywhere, in front of her own house or on her way down the street. We don't know. But, Lucy, we're going to find out. Please believe me. We're going to find whoever it was who murdered your friend."

"Will you? Because nobody's found anything yet," I said.

"We're going to be a lot more thorough now that I'm in charge of the investigation. I'm interviewing everyone who was questioned before, but I'm also going to interview anyone else who might have been home that afternoon, which means we'll be interviewing all the gardeners and housekeepers who didn't get questioned the first time around."

"That sounds great," I said. "Maybe somebody actually saw the car that took her."

Before he left, the lieutenant took photos of the tires of my car. He said they had photographs of the tire tracks around that telephone booth from the day Carmen disappeared, and they were pretty scrambled up and overridden by the police as well as by my Mazda. But they had a program that could sort them out.

Damn! If only I had known…. But how could I have known when I swept my little car around the corner and pulled up alongside that telephone booth that I needed to be careful how I parked that day? I didn't know then it was going to be the worst day of my life. I didn't know then that it was going to be the day I lost Carmen.

CHAPTER 15
MORTIFIED

IT TURNED out Seth *was* a formidable computer hacker, so with his skills, combined with his dad's lax attitude toward computer security, he had easy access to his dad's passwords, and from there, to his dad's data. He really did get a copy of the transcript of my interview by the very next morning, and within a week, Seth had downloaded the entire Carmen case file, including the autopsy and forensic reports, put them on a memory stick, and brought the lot over to my house the following weekend.

I already knew it was going to be rough reading those case files, especially the autopsy and forensic reports, but I wanted to know what was in them. I needed to know. Before Seth got there, I took one of my mom's Valiums. I had been tapering off of them ever since I started back at school and was only taking one or two at night now. But that day I made sure I had a little cushion before I looked at those files. They were only the little 2 mg ones, so I wasn't worried about my judgment being impaired, and I certainly wasn't afraid of falling asleep.

We decided to print out the entire thing all at once to make it easier to collate and share the information between us, so after we let Constanza make us some fresh coffee, we locked the door to my bedroom and went to work. My parents were cool with this. They never questioned my life choices or my work patterns, but just in case, I told Constanza we had an important exam coming up, and we were going to start cramming for it.

First, I uploaded everything from the memory stick into my computer, and then, trying not to read anything yet, I printed out the entire batch. I ran out of ink in the middle, but I had been prepared for this, so I had another cartridge ready, and after a time-out for restarting the printer, it was done. Seth collated everything while I prepared the folders, then we filed them into their separate file folders, and when we were finished, we sat down on the floor, our backs against my bed, and I took a deep breath, and we opened the copy of the autopsy report and started reading.

It was worse than I had ever imagined.

"Oh my God," I moaned. "I forgot there would be photographs!" The first thing I saw was a vivid photo of my beloved Carmen, naked and dead, her skin unnaturally white where it wasn't covered with hideous wounds or purple-and-red bruises. She looked terribly vulnerable and terribly dead, lying on that metal table.

"Maybe you shouldn't look at those," Seth said, clumsily trying to take them out of my hands so that they spilled over my lap and onto the floor, and when I looked down, all I could see were dozens of pictures of my poor Carmen, dead and naked on the metal table with every wound and violation up close and in living (or dead) color. It was all so ghastly, my head began to spin, and I started to feel sick. Then I started to cry.

"Look," Seth said, realizing immediately that it was too much for me, "I think we've seen enough of these. Let's just put them away for now. See? I'm putting them away." And he got down on his knees and gathered them together and slid them upside down inside a file folder.

I was too stunned to go on. "Seth," I said through my tears. "Just read the report to me, okay? I don't think I can look at anything else right now."

"Okay," he said. "I'll just scan this and try to summarize it for you without too much gruesome detail." He took the folder out of my hand and opened it.

"The gist of this autopsy report is that Carmen died of strangulation. She was strangled by hand and not with any device, like a ligature," he said. He stopped and looked over at me, but I just nodded my head for him to continue, because now I knew. Someone had wrung the life out of Carmen with his bare hands!

Seth went ahead with the next part. "Carmen had been raped multiple times." Seth stopped again. "Are you sure you want to know all this?"

I nodded again, but now I just stared down at the rug. "Yes, I need to know," I said finally. "You can go on. I'm all right." But I wasn't really all right. I was thoroughly *not* all right.

"They found evidence of violent rape in every orifice on Carmen's body and they were able to collect DNA from these violations, as well as skin and hair samples." Seth turned to me again. "I'm not going to read any more detail about that. Just that they found three separate specimens of DNA from three separate perpetrators. The medical examiner also states that she was injured so badly and in so many places, both internally and externally, that she might well have died from blood loss due to her injuries if she hadn't been strangled."

"Oh God, my poor Carmen," I moaned.

"She appeared to have been severely beaten, because her face and body were covered with contusions. However, the medical examiner could not determine if all the bruises were caused by physical blows or from being raped in the back of a moving vehicle."

I was sobbing softly now, and Seth went on reading to himself.

"Listen to this, Lucy," Seth said suddenly, looking up from the next part he had been scanning. "Evidently, they've got some machine that uses the latest technology to determine the extent of internal injuries. It says they found evidence of scarring caused by vaginal trauma consistent with an earlier rape! The ME was able to ascertain that Carmen had been raped before, sometime between ten and twelve years of age!"

I began to feel chills then, as if Carmen's ghost was in the room with us, and I thought to myself, so there it is. This is where that rage came from.

"Oh, Seth, I knew it," I said. "I knew something terrible had happened to her when she was a little girl. It was her father! It had to be."

"So Carmen was molested by her own father?"

"Yes, I'm sure of it. That's why she would never talk about him. That's why they don't have any pictures of him at their house. That was what James was trying to tell me!"

I stopped crying then. Somehow, this latest information hardened me. My grief was replaced with hatred and anger at the men who had hurt my beloved. I felt a new resolve to make them pay.

"Are you all right?" Seth asked. "Do you want me to go on? There's only a little bit more."

"I'm fine now. Yes, go on."

"Using that same technology—" Seth stopped just then. "Oh, Lucy, this is even more disgusting than what I've told you so far."

"It's okay," I said. "Go ahead. Read it."

"By carefully studying the ratio of healing and blood loss in the internal injuries in her vagina and rectum, it was determined that Carmen was already dead for a great portion of her attack."

"Oh, that's horrible," I said.

"Whoever they were," Seth added, "they raped and brutalized her body even after she had already died!"

After hearing this last bit, it was impossible to think about reading anything else. All these past months, I had wanted to know exactly what had happened to Carmen, but now that I knew, it was too awful to live with. I wanted to scream. Seth didn't know what to do, either. He didn't know how to comfort me, and honestly, what comfort could anyone offer?

"I think that's enough for one night," he said. "Let's go over to Pips and grab a piece of cheesecake."

I didn't feel like eating anything, but suddenly I felt like I would faint if I didn't get out of that room. "Yes. You're right. Let's go." I practically leapt off the floor and grabbed my black jacket from the desk chair and ran to unlock the door.

"I'll just bring these case notes along just in case," Seth mumbled as he scooped some files up and ran after me.

I let Seth drive and blanked out my mind for the ten minutes it took to get to Westwood Village. We sat in our favorite booth at Pips like two shell-shocked soldiers. The waitress offered us coffee, and we mumbled our thanks. Seth asked if I wanted cheesecake, but I couldn't even summon the strength to pretend this was a social occasion, and I shook my head.

After the waitress came back with our coffee mugs and left us alone again, Seth suggested we move on. "I think we had better leave the next part of the forensics for now. But try to keep what you know in the back of your mind, because any anger you feel is good. It will keep us focused, but we should take a look at some of this other stuff to see if they've made any progress on the case and if they even have any suspects at all."

He opened the top file. "This looks like the list of suspects. Oh, wait, it's not much of a list. It's actually a list of those who have already been ruled out, either by alibi or by obvious nonconnection with Carmen's death—like being black."

"What do you mean?" I asked. "Isn't there a list of suspects?"

"No," Seth said. "They actually don't seem to have any suspects at all."

"Shit," I mumbled. "What's in that next file?"

Seth opened the next file. "It seems to be the forensics' evidence file with the DNA evidence and the findings from the fibers and skin cells and anything else they had gleaned from Carmen's dress or corpse."

"Oh, let's skip that for now," I said, inwardly cringing at the word "corpse." I didn't like to hear that word in relation to my Carmen.

"This next one has all the transcripts from the recent interviews with you and your neighbors, along with a telephone interview with James."

"Is there anything new in there? Do you have time to read them?"

"I can scan my dad's notes. In the new interviews with the neighborhood housekeeping and gardening staff, it looks like a few of them reported seeing a black SUV driving through the neighborhood at the time."

"Lots of our neighbors have black SUVs," I said, disappointed.

"Two housekeepers reported seeing a red SUV in the area," Seth added.

"Well, that's new. Red isn't classy enough for the likes of us. Too garish. So that could be interesting. Any license plates?"

"Sadly, no. No one took note of any license plates."

"Oh well, what's next?"

"Here's a request for footage from the CCTV camera located at the closest exit off the 405 freeway. Whoops, then there's a letter stating that the camera had been broken that week, so the request was turned down. Oh, here's the request for CCTV footage from the private cameras at the residences along your road. There's no reply to that yet."

"Well," I said, "that's a bit more promising. What's next?"

"This file is full of new interviews they conducted with the residents of Malibu in the area near the Pt. Dume Shopping Center next to that part of the Pacific Coast Highway where Carmen's body was discovered."

"Great," I said. "The police questioned those folks last year but hadn't found anything. Maybe your dad's people can turn something up."

"Yeah, it mentions that the CCTV footage from that area had been erased, but they've put in a request for the footage from a service station on the corner of Heathercliff Road, next door to the shopping mall. It says they still have footage from last year."

"Fantastic," I said, sipping the last of my coffee.

"Also, they're still in the process of questioning the residents along Dume Drive and Heathercliff Road too."

"That sounds like a good plan to me," I said, beginning to feel that at least something was being done.

We stopped there. Seth put away the files, and we put down our coffee mugs. I looked across at Seth. He looked tired and worried, and I knew it was my turn to cheer him up.

"Hey, I'm okay now. I'll be all right. I won't sleep tonight with all this coffee, but I'll survive," I said to him, trying to smile. "Thanks for doing all this for me."

"No problem," he answered. "Anytime you want me to drag you through the depths of hell, just give me a call."

"No, really. I needed to know. I'm not sorry. I'm just, I don't know, really shaken by the cruelty and disgustingness of it all. I'm just really shaken." And I felt my resolve begin to crumble, and I was afraid I would start to cry again.

And then Seth did a surprising thing. He got up and came around to my side of the booth and sat down next to me. He put his arms around me and just let me cry on his shoulder. It was a good thing to do. And afterward, I wiped my face with a napkin, and he drove me home.

That night, I put myself to sleep thinking about the folks in Malibu. I thought up a little scenario wherein some nice rich old lady had happened to notice this strange SUV driving around that night, because it was where it ought not to be. In my fantasy, she had actually written down its license plate number and tucked it away on her refrigerator door with a big sunny refrigerator magnet. If only.

CHAPTER 16
STEPHANIE

I MET Seth the next morning before homeroom.

"Hey," he said.

"Hey," I answered.

"How are you doing?" he asked when I climbed out of my car.

"I'm okay. Better," I said.

"Good, 'cause I have some good news to report."

"They didn't catch her killers, did they?"

"Not that good, but the CCTV footage from Malibu arrived at my dad's office last night."

"The footage from the service station on the corner?"

"Yes, from the one on the corner of Pacific Coast Highway and Heathercliff Drive. It was the closest camera to where they had found Carmen's body. The service station had stored all the recordings from the previous year, so they included the timeline between 6:00 p.m. and 8:00 a.m. on that Wednesday night. They also sent along the next day's recordings, just to be on the safe side, so there's loads of footage to review."

"They seem amazingly helpful," I said. "But I guess that's Malibu for you. I just don't understand why the police didn't check them out last year. We're lucky those guys stored the videos."

"Yeah. Well, at least you know my dad's on the ball. The video team are studying them already, but they say it might take them a couple of days to go through it all."

"What about the door-to-door? Did they question the residents in the neighborhood again?" I asked.

"Oh yeah. I read those notes too, but disappointingly, the door-to-door on Heathercliff Drive didn't turn up anything new. No one reported or noted anything unusual that night, and no one saw or heard anything worth remembering."

And, I thought to myself, no one wrote down any license plate numbers to stick onto their refrigerator doors. I was disappointed, but hopeful too, and somehow I made it through another couple of days.

Seth called me Tuesday night to say the video team report was in, and he was going to download it off his dad's computer and bring it to me the next day.

Wednesday morning, Seth met me in the school parking lot with the CCTV report, and we decided to attack it in the privacy of the seniors' lounge after lunch, when we both had a free period.

We'd started using the seniors' lounge pretty regularly as a rendezvous point to go over our notes for what we told everyone else was our special "extra credit" project. Hardly anyone ever used the lounge, so it made a perfect school-day retreat. On the first day we met, when I had brought Seth there, we had agreed to never let any of the kids at the school know his dad was the new captain of the LAPD Homicide Division. We didn't have any particular reason for this secrecy; it just seemed the wise thing to do, and anyway, being the son of a cop was only one step up from being the son of a plumber in our high school pecking order.

We had made up a cover story about his dad being a surgeon like mine, and that was why we knew each other. I couldn't even tell Wendy. We were careful not to let anyone, teacher or student, in on what we were doing. Although, I had to say that since Seth arrived at the school, my mood had greatly improved, so my teachers couldn't help thinking something was up. Happily, they just thought I finally had a boyfriend. It was a good cover for both of us.

We sat at the table in the very back of the lounge now. We'd claimed it as ours for the last several weeks, as it was next to a window, which gave a view out to the student parking lot where our cars were parked, and there were no public areas where students might congregate between our window and our cars.

I brewed a couple of cups of our usual caustic blend, and then Seth opened the report file.

The file was pretty dense, so I let Seth read me the highlights.

"Well, this first part is just the info about the logistics of the footage. There's a description of the camera placement, which was attached to the northeast corner of the roof of the mini-mart," he said, scanning the documents. "It says that the camera provided a twenty-second scan that covered about 180 degrees of the lot, and showed vehicles pulling in and people pumping gas and going inside the mini-mart to pay. Oh, but it also included a view of the road in front of the station. That's Heathercliff Drive." Then he brightened up a bit. "It says that the camera caught an angle to allow visuals of the license plates of vehicles driving to and from the beach."

"That sounds promising," I said, putting our coffee mugs down on the table.

Seth took a long sip of his bitter brew and scanned the next few pages. "The next part of the report is just a list of every license plate of every SUV that could be read, in the lot or on the road. That's it."

"How many numbers is it?" I asked.

"Looks like about fifty."

"That seems like a lot, but I remember it being a particularly balmy day, so a lot of folks were probably driving to the beach that day, or heading home."

"Yeah," agreed Seth, "and being a beach town, a lot of folks around there probably drive SUVs. It says in the round-up notes at the bottom that the video team hadn't seen anything in the tapes that looked suspicious, but they had noted all the license plates anyway, just in case."

"Well, that's a start," I said, feeling a mixture of disappointment and hope. I set to tidying up the lists and putting the report back in its folder. "Do you think it will lead anywhere?"

"Well, I guess it gives them some kind of list to run against any suspects they come up with later," Seth ventured.

"That's true. That's good," I said, but my little shred of hope was beginning to fade inside me again.

"They're still trying to get ahold of the private security CCTV tapes from some of the houses up on your street. That will give them more plates to compare to these—and if any of the same plates turn up in both places, they might have a possible suspect."

"That sounds promising," I said, allowing my shred of hope to revive a bit.

Someone came into the lounge then, so we put the files away and headed for the lunchroom. I was feeling pretty optimistic for the rest of the day.

And then something happened that night that changed everything.

That very night, another girl disappeared. Seth phoned me as soon as he heard his father take the call.

"Lucy," he said, breaking me out of my reverie. I had been lying on my bed listening to a Kristin Hersh album at a crushingly loud volume, which I found strangely comforting. I turned down my stereo.

"Hey," I said, "what's up?"

"Another girl has gone missing. They're not waiting twenty-four hours to pursue the case either. They've already called my dad."

"Oh God," I answered, sitting up. "That's awful. Do we know her?"

"She goes to Uni. Her name is Stephanie Nordstrom. She's a sophomore. Do you know her?"

"I *do* know her. We're not friends or anything, but she's got some of my same teachers. She's supposed to be really intelligent and focused. She's not like the usual entertainment biz brats that go to our school. Her dad is some sort of Swedish diplomat."

"That might account for them taking the case so seriously so quickly. What's she actually like?"

"For one thing, she's gorgeous. You must have seen her walking around campus. She's that sleek and elegant blonde who looks like a supermodel. She's tall enough to be a supermodel, anyway, but she has a really high IQ, and she's totally focused on her music. She plays the violin. She transferred from Pacific Palisades this year because Uni has a better orchestra. She couldn't care less about the boys in our school, because she still has a boyfriend at Palisades High."

"I've definitely seen her. She's that icy blonde who's always carrying a violin case."

"She'd be pretty hard to miss," I said. "What's happened to her?"

"According to the report I've already copied," Seth said, "she disappeared on her way to her Wednesday-evening violin lesson. Her violin tutor only lives two houses up the road from Stephanie in Laurel Canyon. It takes less than five minutes to walk there, and evidently she's made that five-minute walk every Wednesday for the last two years, ever since her family moved to LA. When she didn't show up, the tutor called her parents. She's never missed a lesson in her life, and her parents were frantic."

"I bet," I said. "So what are they doing about it?"

"Her parents called missing persons as soon as they checked with Stephanie's boyfriend to make sure she wasn't with him," Seth said. "Missing persons contacted my dad immediately, because of Carmen's case. I guess because both girls went to the same high school. But there's another similarity, Lucy," Seth added. "The team noticed that today is Wednesday, the same day of the week that Carmen had been taken."

"So even though it started out as a missing persons' case, the police are expecting the worst," I finished for him.

"Yeah, sorry," Seth said.

"You know," I said, "there are a lot of other similarities between those girls. Even though I don't know Stephanie very well, I do know that she is gorgeous, just like Carmen was. Looking the way she did, the same guys were always hitting on her, but she turned everyone down, of course, just like Carmen. She had this amazing confidence bordering on arrogance, which I thought was totally cool, especially when I saw her in action. She wasn't concerned about what the jocks at Uni High thought about her. She was completely focused on her future as a concert violinist. God, she was beautiful, brilliant, and talented. I thought she had everything going for her."

"Sadly, none of those wonderful attributes are going to save her, unless the police find her first." Seth said.

"That's awful," I said. "I hope they find her before it's too late."

"Look, I'll keep you posted with anything I hear tonight, okay?"

"That would be great, because I don't think I'll be getting any sleep tonight anyway. Feel free to call me whenever you hear anything. Anything at all. And Seth, thank you for letting me know."

Seth kept his word and called me throughout the night with up-to-the-minute reports of how Stephanie hadn't been found yet, so I didn't get much sleep. Then, just as I was forcing myself out of bed at 7:30 a.m. to get ready for school, Seth called me one last time.

"Lucy," he said, pausing strangely. I could tell from the way he said my name that he had bad news to report. So I sat back down on my bed.

"Yeah," I answered, and waited for him to break the news.

"She's dead."

"Oh no," I said, and for some reason I burst out crying. "What happened?"

"They found her body this morning. She'd been dumped off the Ventura Freeway sometime during the night. A dog walker spotted her body near the Studio City exit early this morning."

"Oh, I'm so sorry," I sobbed. "Did you hear anything more?"

"Not yet, but my dad is definitely on the case. It's officially a homicide. Will you be okay?"

"Yes, I don't know why I'm crying. I hardly knew her."

"It's okay. Will you make it to school all right?"

"Yeah. I'll be all right. I'll see you in the usual place. Thanks."

I hung up and went into my bathroom and washed my face. I thought about waking my mom and talking to her about Stephanie, but decided I could handle it. I didn't even need a Valium. I'd be better once I saw Seth.

I met Seth in the parking lot as usual. The story had broken on the news by the time I got there, so most everyone knew about Stephanie's murder already. Seth had been handed a leaflet advising us that everyone was to come to the school auditorium for a special assembly. So we headed over there. The student body filed in, all teary-eyed and anxious, but Seth and I hung back so we could make our escape as soon as the assembly was over.

The principal greeted the student body but left it to the vice principal to inform us of what had officially happened to Stephanie and to remind us to be cautious and to never go anywhere alone—to always have a buddy. My buddy was Seth. We were already sitting together at the back. Then the school counselor informed us that she had set up some kind of counseling center in the nurse's office, in case anyone felt traumatized by the brutal murder of a fellow classmate. I was still traumatized by the brutal murder of my best friend, but I didn't want any counseling. I only wanted revenge.

CHAPTER 17
SHAKESPEARE'S

CLASSES WERE cancelled for the rest of the day, so Seth and I had nothing else to do while we waited for whatever news he could glean from his father's computer. Neither of us wanted to go home, so I suggested he come with me to Shakespeare's.

I hadn't been to Shakespeare's since the day Carmen disappeared. I simply hadn't been able to face it. I knew everyone there would have heard about her murder, and they would have been kind and sympathetic to me, but I didn't think I could handle their kindness and sympathy at the time. After a while, I felt embarrassed to return after I'd stayed away for so long. But ever since Seth and I became friends, I'd wanted to take him there. I knew he would like it, and I knew Cedric and Sebastian would like Seth.

Shakespeare's was always open, even at ten o'clock in the morning, so I had Seth follow me in his Honda through the downtown Santa Monica traffic, all the way to the edge of Venice, where Shakespeare's was. The parking lot was pretty empty that early in the morning, so we were able to park up against the guitar store, and I led Seth to the secret door at the back. Well, it really wasn't so secret because there was a brightly colored sign above the door with the name Shakespeare's in psychedelic lettering, but you would never know the club was there unless someone told you about it.

"So this is it?" Seth said, looking up at the sign as I opened the door.

We made our way down the stairs carefully, because it took our eyes a while to adjust to the dim light after the bright morning outside. As my eyes adjusted, I began to recognize an old song playing dreamily on the house stereo. I couldn't remember the title, but it was by a band called Country Joe and the Fish. I think my dad owned the same album.

Sebastian was doing the morning shift, and he spotted us as soon as we reached the last step. I think he had been dancing to the music as he cleaned the tables because he waved his washcloth at us now as if it were Diana Ross's ermine stole.

"My, my," he said, beaming over at me, "the prodigal daughter returns."

Then he came right up and gave me a big, embarrassing hug. "We missed you, Lucy," he whispered. Then he let me go and looked over at Seth. "And who, may I ask, is this?"

"Sebastian, this is Seth. Seth, Sebastian. He owns the place," I announced.

"Cedric and I own this wonderful club together. It's nice to meet you, Seth." And he shook Seth's hand and smiled from ear to ear. Sebastian was quite tall and lean, and he still wore his red hair very long, although it was usually tied back in a ponytail or a braid like it was today. He also sported a full beard. He still dressed like a hippie too, wearing bell-bottom pants, flowing shirts, and a lot of jewelry and scarves. He was always wonderfully jolly, kind of like a redheaded hippie Santa Claus.

Seth looked around the place, taking it all in, the little café tables, the bookshelves, the small stage, and the sleeping young people on the back benches. Even though it was pretty early, there were several couples sitting at the tables, sipping coffee and talking to each other in low voices. As usual, they were mostly boys, and a lot of them were holding hands and looking at each other with love-filled eyes.

"Want some coffee?" Sebastian asked. "A brownie?"

"Actually, yes," Seth said, blinking his eyes against the vision of the array of brownies set out on little round trays on the counter. "A brownie would be nice."

"Seth's always hungry," I said. "Just coffee for me, though. Can I light my candle?" I asked, sitting down at one of the tables he had just cleaned and digging for a lighter in my handbag. I liked having the candles lit. I liked the atmosphere of the place, with its candles and sweet smell of patchouli oil, and of course, I liked the coffee.

"How do you take your coffee, Seth?"

"Can I get a latte?" he asked, spying the espresso machine. Carmen and Seth both took cream and sugar in their coffee, but if they could get a latte, that was their preferred beverage.

"Sure," said Sebastian. "No problem."

Seth sat down across from me but kept looking around the room. I think the presence of the gay boys was sinking in, because when he faced me, he had kind of a confused expression on his bony face. Fortunately, Sebastian walked over just then with a tray for our drinks and a plate of brownies for Seth.

"Thanks," I said, sipping the wonderful coffee. It was French roast, my favorite, so much better than that chemical brew I made for us at school. Seth sipped his latte and raised his eyebrows.

"This is good," he said appreciatively. He picked up a brownie, but he just stared at it for a moment like he was afraid it might be filled with marijuana or something. Then he sniffed it. I had to admit they smelled great, and I could see Seth figured it was safe to take a bite because he stuffed a huge piece into his mouth and munched. "This is good too," he said after he swallowed. Then he looked at me with that confused expression again. "So," he said finally. "This is the famous Shakespeare's."

"Well, it's not exactly famous," I answered. "Just the opposite. I think that's why I like it."

"So that's the reason you like it? Not because it's a gay hangout?"

There it was, then. The cat coming out of the bag. I didn't know what to say to that, so I didn't say anything at all and just took another sip of my coffee, but I met his gaze, which was kind of hard to do, because his eyes were suddenly a lot darker than I was used to.

"So do you think I'm gay?" he asked. He took another bite of his brownie and continued to look at me darkly.

"Well, you know, *I'm* gay," I told him, because I actually didn't know if he knew that about me. I mean, we'd talked about how much I loved Carmen, but I never said anything about *how* I loved Carmen or how she loved me.

"You are?"

"Don't tell me you didn't guess?" I said.

"I never thought about it. But you haven't answered my question. Do *you* think *I'm* gay?"

"I don't know, are you?"

"Do you want me to be?"

"Actually, I was kind of hoping you were. Are you?"

Seth put down the last bit of his brownie and sat back in his chair, thrusting his long legs into the aisle at the side of the table. He chewed on his lower lip as if he were actually thinking about it. I began to wonder if I had guessed wrong. I don't know why I thought he might be gay. Oh yes, I did. He was too nice and too sensitive to be anything else. And he'd never tried to make a move on me either. Plus, I'd never heard him talk about any girls in his past, and he never remarked on the looks of any member of our female student body, no matter how scantily clad they were. He was different from any boy I'd ever known. Besides, it was true: I *wanted* him to be gay.

"Actually, Lucy, I don't know."

"That's exactly what Carmen and I said the first time we came here. We didn't know either."

"But you do now?"

"Yes, that's right. I know I'm gay now. Don't tell me you never suspected it or anything?"

"No, not really. You don't look gay."

"Oh? What does that mean?" I said, unexpectedly offended. "I'm not wearing a buzz cut? I'm not butch enough?"

"Well, I guess...."

"Honestly, I don't understand that anyway. Why would I want to look like a boy when I don't even like boys?"

"You said you liked me."

"Okay. You're right. I don't dislike men *or* boys. I just don't want them as sexual partners, and I have no desire to look like one or to have my lovers look like one."

"You have lovers?"

"No, I was just thinking about Carmen. She was so feminine, so womanly. I loved her."

Seth leaned forward now and stretched his long arms across the table. "It's all right if you're gay. I like you the way you are, and if gay is the way you are, then I like that too."

I breathed a sigh of relief and took his hands in both of mine, amazed at how big his hands felt and how long his fingers were. Carmen's hands were so small, like mine.

"That's nice to know," I said.

"So, the answer is simply that I don't know about me yet," he said. "I'm kind of a late bloomer."

"You're seventeen years old," I said.

"Yes, but I haven't had time to think about my sexual orientation, Lucy. I'm definitely not ready to declare."

"Well, then, that's okay too," I assured him. "I like you the way you are, whatever way that is."

CHAPTER 18
THE MURDER BOARD

AFTER WE finished our coffee, we said good-bye to Sebastian and walked back up the stairs to our separate cars. Then we each drove home to our own houses. I needed to talk to my mom about Stephanie, and Seth promised to keep an eye on the police reports and call me as soon as any important reports came through.

Stephanie's autopsy report came in later that night, and Seth phoned me as soon as he saw it, then printed off a copy and drove right over to my house. We locked ourselves in my bedroom again and studied the report.

It was just as horrific as Carmen's murder, only this time there was only evidence of *two* perpetrators.

"That's interesting," I told Seth.

"Yes, and this time both perpetrators are in the system. They have the same DNA profile as Carmen's killers," Seth announced.

"So it was definitely not only, as they say, the same MO, it was the same exact guys, minus one!" I was on to something now, even though it didn't make Stephanie's murder any more palatable.

Seth, sensibly, hadn't printed out the photos this time, but the report described the savage attack on Stephanie in the same gruesome detail as Carmen's report. Stephanie had been brutally raped and beaten, and every part of her body had undergone some horrific abuse. She had also been strangled at some point during the ordeal. Once again, using the most modern technology, and judging by the time of death and the nature of her wounds and the body's healing ratio, etc., it was determined she was already dead when half the rape had taken place. It was sickening and difficult to read, but then a little light shone at the end of the findings that made us think perhaps we were moving closer to finding her killers.

"Look at this, Lucy!" Seth pointed at the last lines of the report. "Evidently, Stephanie managed to put up a pretty good fight. Both her arms were broken in the struggle, but the coroner found not only the perpetrators' skin under her fingernails, they found bits of hair and skin in her teeth."

"She bit one of them!" I yelled. "Fantastic!"

A few minutes later, we had all the case files from both murders laid out across my two beds. I had taken the chalkboard out of the rumpus room and set it up between the windows in my bedroom, and I was standing beside it with a piece of chalk, ready to start our own "murder board."

"Let's go over what we know are the facts," Seth said wisely.

I drew a line down the middle of the board, from top to bottom, and wrote CARMEN on the left side and STEPH on the right. "Okay," I began. "Here are the two victims. Should we start with what they had in common?"

"Yeah." And Seth walked over and stood on the other side of the chalkboard. "I'll fill in Steph's side, and you do Carmen's."

"Okay, well, let's start with Wednesday night, then. They were both abducted and murdered on a Wednesday night," I said, and we both wrote WEDNESDAY in our columns.

"New to school?" offered Seth.

"Yeah, I guess. They both started school as sophomores in the fall." And I wrote NEW TO SCHOOL and then SOPHOMORE on Carmen's side, and Seth did the same for Stephanie.

"And neither of the girls dated boys at our school," added Seth.

"That is very true—and both were attractive and turned down a lot of guys."

"Okay, now we are getting somewhere." Seth grinned, and he wrote BEAUTIFUL in my column and BEAUTIFUL in his, and then added DID NOT DATE in his, and I wrote that in mine also.

I couldn't think of anything else, so I stood back and stared at the chart until something came to me. Seth put down his chalk and did the same.

"Hmmm. Not a lot to go on."

I stared at the words for a while, and then something clicked. "Isn't Wednesday night the only day in the week that there isn't a football practice?"

"Yeah. I think you're right. They never have sports practice on Wednesdays because games are always on Fridays. They have a heavy practice on Monday and Tuesday nights and sometimes on the weekend, but they take Wednesday off, have a minipractice on Thursday, and the big game is always on Friday."

"So, it could be possible that these creeps are actually on our football team. They could actually go to our school!"

"That's crazy! Murderers and rapists, especially brutal ones like these, don't just go to some middle-class high school like this! They're gonna be real criminals, probably from Compton."

"Look, we already know that the killers are white guys, from the hairs found on Carmen and from the skin in Stephanie's mouth. Plus, they're not in the system, so they are not known criminals."

So I added WHITE KILLERS to my Carmen list, and Seth took up the chalk and wrote the same in his column.

"And now you're thinking that they're jocks going to our school?"

"That's exactly what I'm thinking." And I wrote JONNY FREEMAN on Carmen's side of the board, then moved over some papers and sat down on the bed and just stared at his name.

"What does that mean? Who's Jonny Freeman?"

"Listen, Seth. Do you remember when I told you about that guy who thought he saw Carmen in the backseat of his car when he rolled it off the edge of Bellagio Road last year? That's Jonny Freeman! He nearly died in an accident he said was caused by seeing Carmen's ghost. He's been in the hospital ever since. Now, six months later, two guys kidnap and murder a girl in the same way that three guys kidnapped and murdered Carmen last year, before Jonny Freeman was out of commission."

"And now you're thinking that Jonny Freeman is the third guy in Carmen's murder? And he and his creepy friends on the football team are responsible?"

"That's exactly what I'm thinking. Is there any way we can get your dad to swipe him for some DNA?"

"They'll have lots of DNA at that hospital he's in, but I don't know if we have enough evidence to convince my dad to get a search warrant."

"Well, then, we'll have to work on that. See if we can come up with something to convince him."

"But there's something else that we can use too, that I just remembered," Seth said, brightening up. He got up and walked over to the chalkboard again. "Stephanie took a sizable chunk out of someone's arm. Whoever it is, they're going to be wounded. We need to take a good look at any guy wearing a large bandage on his arm!" Then he added WOUNDED PERP on Stephanie's side of the board.

"Brilliant!"

"But it's not going to be easy to find someone with a bandage and accuse him of being a rapist," Seth added. "First of all, those guys on the football team are usually pretty heavily taped up, especially their wrists. They've always got their forearms covered in bandages. And, even if whoever it is doesn't get taped up, he's probably wise enough to know that this bite will incriminate him, so he'll tape himself up so he looks like the others or he'll wear a long-sleeved shirt to school."

"Yeah, that's true, but maybe we can see them before they get taped up before a game. You're a guy, maybe you can go into the locker room and see them when they're dressing."

"You must be crazy! I can't go into the locker room when those jocks are in there. Do you want to get me killed too?"

"Okay, I see your point." I sat back down on the bed and thought. "Let's see what we can do, from a purely investigative viewpoint."

"Wait a minute!" Seth brightened up. "I think I've got part of a plan."

"And what's that?" I asked.

"Well, it's a two-parter." He sat down on the floor in front of the bed. "Part one is this: all sports injuries that require medical attention of any kind, including just antiseptic and a Band-Aid, have to be reported to the school administration—and logged in to the nurse's accident report logs. I'm not sure whether they have those on the computer yet. They may only keep the log on a clipboard, but that's probably hanging in the nurse's office somewhere. I can hack into the school computer, but it might be easier for one of us to just get sick and go to the nurse's office and look for ourselves. That will rule out the real injuries, anyway."

"Okay, so what's the second part?"

"I just realized that I might be able to get into the locker room without getting beaten up."

"And how exactly is that going to happen?"

"Baseball tryouts are starting."

"Yes, and?"

"I never told you this about me—'cause you know, we only just started hanging out, but—" He paused. "You know I'm not a jock, right?"

"Yeah, right."

"What I didn't tell you is that I'm kind of a good baseball player. I was kind of the starting pitcher on our school's baseball team in Austin."

"Kind of?" Seth was standing in front of the chalkboard now, and seeing his shy, lanky posture, I could suddenly see it.

"You're some kind of a baseball star, and you never told me?"

"Look, I'm *not* a jock! I just have this knack. Baseball's really popular in Austin, and I started out in little league!"

I had to forgive him now. My own brother was in little league. Baseball was in a special category for a team sport. It was one of the few sports that did not require brawn. In fact, you didn't have to be big at all, and it certainly helped to be a quick thinker, and a little agility went a long way. I had also heard that height in a pitcher was a definite advantage.

"Okay! I believe you, and I forgive you for not telling me."

"And you don't think I'm a jock?"

"And I don't think you're a jock—'cause if you are, you are the nerdiest jock I've ever met!"

"Great, that's settled. Now, let's see if I can hack into the injury log, if they have one."

"And if you can't, I might get a migraine or something and have to go to the nurse's office next week."

"Right." So I stood up and wrote a few more things on the murder board. I wrote JOCKS on both sides and INJURED PLAYER on Stephanie's side.

I felt pretty good about all this. Like maybe we were getting closer to finding them. I really wanted to go to Seth's father with our murder board suspicions, but Seth convinced me we should wait and see what else we could pick up in the coming week that would enable homicide to get a search warrant for Jonny Freeman's DNA.

That night, I put myself to sleep plotting our next moves.

CHAPTER 19
THE NEW COACH

SETH WAS no slacker, and that very night, he hacked into the nurse's office computer and looked to see if he could view any of the nurse's logs, but there didn't seem to be any info for sports injuries there, nor was there anything in the administration's computers, the sports department's, or the physical education computer. So, on Monday, I developed a god-awful migraine and had to go to the nurse's office and lie down. She was terribly sweet when I told her I just needed to rest in a darkened room for a while, and it was all right with me if she wanted to sneak out for a cup of tea in the teacher's lounge.

When she was gone, I looked around her office, and I found the sports' log right away because it was hanging on a nail on the back of the door—and I also found the photocopier, so I ran off a quick copy of all injuries suffered since school had begun this fall. I stuffed one copy into my jeans pocket and lay back down and studied the other.

I didn't find what I had expected, but what I did find was exceedingly curious. Among the normal stream of sports injuries caused by the overly zealous use of force on the playing field, or the too-strenuous workouts on the practice field, the number of cheerleading injuries drew my attention. They began popping up with unusual regularity. Right after the tryouts ended and the school year began, the cheerleading team started showing up in the nurse's office with one injury after another. There were many more than I would have expected and a lot more than Wendy had come to know about. They were mostly bumps and bruises in the beginning, requiring only ice and arnica, but they seemed to get progressively more serious in the next month, beginning with a dislocated shoulder, followed by a broken collarbone, and then Natalie's black eye.

I didn't know why, but these injuries made me feel as if something was more wrong with the cheerleading squad than a few new routines would warrant, and I desperately wanted to know more. I decided I would somehow enlist Wendy's help to see if she could get one of her friends, like that Caroline person, to confide in her.

I stayed in the nurse's office, napping for most of the afternoon, and then met up with Seth at the end of the day. We decided to go to Pip's again, and we ate cheesecake and drank coffee while we studied the nurse's log and made a list of the real football injuries. There actually were far too many injuries for the list to be of any use, but as we went through the log, Seth noticed the cheerleader injuries right away.

"What's this all about? Here's a broken wrist on one girl, there's a broken collarbone on another girl, Natalie gets a black eye, and this girl Claudia complains of hearing loss—after she says she smacked her head on the mat during practice? It sounds to me like the girls are beating each other up!"

"I was going to mention that. I thought that looked strange too. Something's going on. They all say it's just the new routines, but this is the first year anything like this has happened. My friend Wendy knows some of the girls on the squad, and she's even getting worried about it. She says they're all starting to look depressed—which I don't think is a good thing for a cheerleader."

"I don't know how it ties in with the football team, but the two usually go together—cheerleaders and football players...."

"Yeah. So I'm going to do a little investigation of my own on that score. I'm going to talk to Wendy again and see if she can find out any more from her friends on the squad."

"Good idea. So, why don't we start looking at the football team seriously. Maybe you can tell me what you know about Jonny's friends on the team? If we make Jonny Freeman our focus, he should lead us to the other suspects. It makes sense if we figure that he was really the third guy, then we could follow his connections to find the other two guys."

"Okay. Firstly, Jonny wasn't on the football team. He was a track star—a sprinter who also ran the hurdles, and from what I heard, he was pretty amazing. But he didn't hang out with the track team. Basically, they weren't cool enough for him. He liked to hang out with the football team, probably because that was where all the hot girls were. And he didn't hang out with just anyone on the team; he hung out with the school's star quarterback, Luke Ritter."

"Hey, I've seen that Luke character around the school. He's pretty hunky."

"Yeah, he's definitely got the looks: chiseled face, lopsided grin, and those baby blues." I couldn't help but grin at Seth. "You don't have to be ashamed. He's incredibly attractive to nearly every girl *and* guy in the school."

It was true; with his good looks and his Muscle Beach physique, he was a major heartthrob. He could also throw the football amazing distances, with laser-beam accuracy. He was generally recognized as a phenomenal player, and that's how he earned his nickname "Skywalker." I never paid any attention to football, but even I couldn't help noticing him and his buddies leaning against the railings or striding around the school, laughing at their inside jokes or picking on one of the nerds.

I filled Seth in on the recent history of our football team, which fittingly went by the name of the Wildcats. "It is pretty much agreed that our school has a remarkable football team, not only because we are number one in our division, but because we are number one without having any black players on our team."

"Yes, I kind of noticed that you don't have very much variety in color at your school."

"This is because there aren't many kids of color in our neighborhood!" I answered. "Well, actually, there are a few, but they're all just middle-class nerds, and the blackest thing these kids do is play trumpet and saxophone in the school band." Seth laughed, and I went on.

"University High has traditionally been more famous for its marching band than for its football team, and has always spent more money on the orchestra and the auditorium than on the sports facilities. But the story changed two years ago, when certain alumni of the dot-com generation made a concentrated effort to raise the school's sports profile. They hired this big-time coach from a Midwest junior college who came with a reputation for putting his school on the sports map, especially the football team. His name is Coach Billy, Billy Boehm, and he's the biggest ego on campus.

"So in one year, he transformed our football team from the biggest losers in LA County to the first-place winners in our division. We became the most talked-about high school team in the LA area. Everyone thought the coach was so great that those same wealthy alumni paid his salary for the next four years. The gossip in the girls' room is that he is a total brute who drives the players hard, has a foul mouth, and doesn't take no for an answer. Maybe you've seen him in the halls? He's kind of big and bulky looking but fit, with a big square head, weather-beaten face, and thick silver-gray hair that I am sure he dyes. He's always dressed in light blue jeans, the kind they call 'easy fit' for big guys, and a light blue Levi's jacket. Evidently, he works Luke, the quarterback, especially hard, but they seem to be buddies, which is interesting, come to think of it…. But Luke's arm just gets better and better, so he must be doing something right, or so everyone thinks.

"Rumor around school is that we always beat the other teams because we always *beat* the other teams, literally. The few losses we suffer are caused by penalties for 'unnecessary roughness,' and there is always a lot of fighting on and off the field. Our team took a lot of penalties for roughing up the passer, etcetera, last year—and pulling all kinds of unsportsmanlike shit on the field."

Seth interrupted me then. "Even around the school, the players seem to be always hyped up. They positively stalk around campus, not just as if they owned the place, but like it was their own little kingdom! I certainly try to stay out of their way. You know what I think?"

"What?"

"I think that this hotshot coach is feeding the team steroids!"

"Now that *is* interesting. That would explain a lot."

"We've got a lot of that going around in Texas, as you'd expect, since everything is supposed to be bigger in Texas. If your kid's not growing fast enough, you get him some steroids. It's still illegal and dangerous for underage boys."

"And even I know that steroids can cause behavioral changes and aggressiveness! That would explain all these increased injuries and penalties for aggression on the field."

"Plus, it has lots of other unappetizing side effects. It really makes me wonder...."

"So, now we've got something else to consider as well. It just convinces me more and more that the football team is going to be where we find our killers." And then I looked at Seth's eager but still geeky face plotting away across the booth from me, and I added, "But the more I think about it, the more worried I get about the danger we could be getting ourselves into. Especially you."

"But the tryouts for the baseball team are this Saturday. I'm not going to back down. I'm still willing to be the inside man."

"What are your chances of making the team, seriously?" I asked.

"Seriously? I've been watching the other guys practicing. It's going to be a cakewalk. But just remember, I'm not a jock. I just have this talent. You'll see. Anyway, I'll be in the locker room tomorrow 'cause we'll be warming up before the tryouts start."

"Please be careful. I'll be cheering for you, but only if you promise not to get yourself killed."

"Don't worry, I won't be a hero," he promised. "I'll just be your inside man."

CHAPTER 20
MY INSIDE MAN

SETH'S COVER turned out to be pretty phenomenal, because he stunned everyone, including me, with his performance on the baseball diamond at the tryouts. He hadn't been exaggerating; he really was an incredible pitcher. It was obvious even to me. I was watching from the bleachers, a place I had never thought I would find myself. He was so amazing the baseball coach didn't hesitate to make him the starting pitcher on the spot. I think the baseball coach was so shocked at his good fortune he snapped Seth up before Seth could think twice about it.

When I told my family about Seth's surprising baseball prowess, my brother and his friends were over the moon, thinking I had an actual baseball star for a boyfriend. From that day forth, whenever Seth came over to our house, he would immediately be hijacked into tossing baseballs around the backyard, so we had to dedicate a precious half hour to pleasing the kids before we could get down to the serious business of solving Carmen's murder.

Anyway, Seth had been right; making the team had been a cakewalk, and now that he was an instant baseball star, he had the perfect inside ticket to the locker room.

"You won't believe it, Lucy," Seth told me at Pips after only a week of baseball practice. "Those jocks just love me. Even the football players love me."

"Well, everybody loves America's favorite pastime," I said, digging in to a fat slice of cheesecake. I was hungry again, now that we were doing something constructive.

"The players are not only talking to me, but they actually seem to be talking to me with respect."

"You mean they're not just snapping towels at you," I said, secretly pleased.

"All this attention is going to take some getting used to," Seth confided. "Those guys on the football team are pretty intimidating. The sheer size of them is terrifying."

"Are you safe?" I asked. "Do they seem dangerous? You said they liked you."

"Yeah, they like me. I'm fine. They just make me feel puny."

"Well, you are pretty skinny, even if you are tall," I said. It was true. Although Seth was at least six feet tall, that was far below average height for the football team, and a lot of those guys, including Skywalker, were over six foot four and hugely muscular, weighing in at over two hundred pounds. "How much do you weigh?" I asked, looking up from my cheesecake, which I was mashing with my fork for some reason.

"Last time I weighed myself was in the nurse's office last week. I weighed in at around 155 with all my clothes on."

"Well, then, you *are* puny!" I said, laughing into a forkful of cheesecake.

"That's not funny," he grumbled.

"Well, what's your plan, anyway?" I asked.

"I've been taking my time dressing so I'm still in the locker room when the football team finishes practice. That way I get to listen in on their chatter, which is usually pretty revolting, mainly about who they smashed that day and who they were going to screw that night."

"Ugh. Poor you," I sympathized. "Have you found out anything interesting besides who they're screwing?" I asked.

"Well, one thing I've noticed right away is that Coach Billy seems to be far too buddy-buddy with some of the players, especially Luke and some of the bigger receivers, like Carl Brandt. They hang out together after practice. The way they talk about girls is even creepier than normal jock talk. Also, when the coach is in the locker room, there seems to be a lot of hush-hush, wink-wink going on, like they couldn't talk out loud if I was in the room."

"Interesting," I said. "I wonder what's going on."

"My guess is it's the steroids," said Seth. "But I haven't seen any yet."

In the second week of baseball practice, Seth started noticing something that really made him suspicious and uncomfortable.

"Have you ever seen the coach's new office?" he asked me during our free period. We were in the seniors' lounge enjoying a cup of chemical brew.

"I've seen the outside of it. I've never been inside," I answered.

When Coach Billy came to our school, the alumni had a special office built for him in a separate building attached to the PE department. It was situated between the boys' locker room and the gym.

"I heard it was supposed to be pretty snazzy, as offices go," I added.

"Yes, that's what I hear," said Seth. "But why does he need a separate building? The other coaches share offices inside the PE building itself, but Coach Billy has a whole separate building with its own entrance from the field walkway between the gym and the locker room."

"I guess it's just to show what a big wheel he is," I said.

"He's got a separate entrance into the PE building too. Anyway, since I've been there, I've seen the players flowing pretty freely in and out of his office. And you know who else?" Seth set down his mug of bitter brew and looked at me with raised eyebrows.

"No," I answered. "I don't. Who else?"

"Cheerleaders," he said, "that's who else."

"Tell me more," I said, feeling suddenly dizzy.

"When I'm warming up in the batter's box, I can see the coach's office door. It opens onto the walkway between the field and the gym. The batter's box is just on the other side of the walkway. I have a good view of the gym entrance and the coach's door."

"And?" I said, anxious to know what he was getting at.

"You know that cheerleading practice takes place after school nearly every day. Well, I'm around most every day too. They work out inside the gym, and after practice the cheerleaders usually hang around for a while. Sometimes they watch the baseball practice, but mostly they're just waiting for their football hunk boyfriends to finish *their* practice."

"And?" I asked, growing impatient.

"Well, this week, I began to notice some of the cheerleaders actually going inside the coach's office after practice. I never see them come out, but I figure they must use the inside door into the PE building, but still, what were they doing inside the coach's office in the first place?"

"Yes, exactly," I agreed. "What were the cheerleaders doing in the football coach's office?"

"Then yesterday afternoon, I saw two cheerleaders arguing outside the gym, between the two buildings. One of the girls started to cry, and the other girl pulled her back inside the gym. Five minutes later, they both came out. The girl who had been crying looked like she had washed her face and put on more makeup. They talked outside for a few seconds, and then I saw the other girl push the girl who had been crying toward the coach's office. She left her there and walked back inside the gym. I watched the other girl. She just stood in front of the coach's door, staring at it for at least two minutes, but then I saw her finally knock on the door, and when it opened, she walked right in. I never saw *her* come out either."

"That's very weird," I said. "*And* it doesn't sound good."

"That's what I thought," said Seth. "It doesn't sound very healthy."

"That's putting it delicately," I said, feeling nauseous.

A FEW days later, Seth got a breakthrough in our steroid investigation. He called me from his car as soon as he left the gym and told me the whole story.

It seemed that Carl Brandt, one of the running backs, a big, beefy guy who liked baseball a lot, sidled up to Seth that day when they were alone in the locker room.

"Hey, hotshot," he said, smiling warmly at Seth. He'd been friendly to Seth ever since the baseball tryouts had revealed Seth's amazing curve ball. "How'd you like to improve your batting average?"

"Why?" Seth asked. "Do you think I have a problem?"

Carl just laughed. "Whoa, there, hotshot, everybody can use improvement. Look at how well the football team does. Not one loss all season."

"So what's the secret? What do I need to do to make me a better hitter?" Seth asked.

Carl took a little bottle out of his pocket and showed Seth these little white pills.

"What are those? Some kind of speed, Dexedrine or something?" Seth asked, pretending ignorance.

"No way, man, this is the real deal. 'Roids, man. Steroids." Carl laughed again and slapped Seth on the back.

"So, like, do all of you take them?" Seth asked.

"Pretty much the whole team. I gained twenty-five pounds of pure muscle since I started on them. I used to be kind of weedy like you," Carl said.

"Golly," said Seth, wondering what to say next. "Well, like, how much do they cost—and what's the deal? Don't I need to do something to make them work?"

"Nah," answered Carl. "You just take one of these little pills in the morning and go to your regular baseball practice and do your workouts like a good little boy, and you'll see the change. You'll have more energy, you'll be able to throw faster, and you'll be able to hit the ball harder in no time!"

"So, where do you get them, man? Aren't they illegal?"

"Come on, hotshot, don't give me that, you smoke dope, don't you?"

When Seth told me this, all I could think was "As if!" Poor Seth wouldn't dare bring drugs into his house, not with random drug testing in the police department. Even Seth's dad could be tested at random intervals, and just a whiff of marijuana could wind up in his dad's bloodstream. Seth would never compromise his dad's career.

But he answered, "Yeah, of course."

"Well, we have a good supplier, and we get a good deal. I can get you a thirty-day supply for just one hundred dollars."

"But how can you be sure this is the right stuff? They just look like little white pills to me."

"See, man, this is the stuff the coach has us use. He knows the right stuff, and he gets it medical grade!"

"Wow." Seth tried to look enthusiastic. "Let me think about it. I don't have much left in my allowance."

"Well, don't wait too long." Carl slapped Seth fondly on his skinny backside and left the locker room.

CHAPTER 21
TIME TO ACT

"WELL, THAT should be enough, shouldn't it?" I asked Seth that evening. "I think it's time for me to talk to your dad before something else awful happens." We were at Pips again, eating cheesecake and drinking our usual endless mugs of coffee. "I don't think it's wise to wait any longer."

Lately, we'd made a habit of meeting at Pip's every evening after baseball practice so Seth could give me the rundown on his undercover work and to plan our next steps.

"Don't let's get ahead of ourselves," he warned me. "That's not what the police would call evidence." He put down his fork and looked at me without a trace of a smile. "I haven't worn a wire, so it's all what they call 'hearsay' and not admissible in court. And besides, it only means that the coach is a drug dealer, not a murderer."

"But at least we know for a fact that there is something definitely rotten in the Uni High School locker room and that Coach Billy is probably behind it. Shouldn't that be enough to raise a warrant, or at least suspicions?" I said, disappointed. "I mean, it's all beginning to make sense now. We already know that football is a brutal sport, especially the way our team plays it, but with steroids involved, it looks more and more as if some of our players carried out those brutal attacks."

"But why?" Seth asked. "Why kidnap and rape when they could get any girl in the school they wanted?"

"Oh, but that's just it. They couldn't get Carmen or Stephanie. Neither of those girls would give any of those guys the time of day, football heroes or not. And remember, rape isn't really a sexual act; it's more about power—and maybe about anger? Maybe their egos couldn't handle the rejection. But I don't really care why they did it; all I want is to get some detectives down there to investigate, and pronto!'

It had been three weeks since Stephanie's murder and two weeks into Seth's undercover locker-room ordeal. I knew there was a lot more to be learned, but time was slipping away, and now, with the addition of the cheerleaders' inexplicable behavior, we needed to catch whomever was responsible before someone else got hurt—or worse!

"You may be right. You probably are right. It's all beginning to make a kind of disgusting sense," Seth said, looking up from where he was neatly separating the filling from the graham-cracker crust of his cheesecake. "Carl is expecting me to buy into the steroids, and I don't know how I'm supposed to stall him. I'm not really an undercover cop. I don't want to act more suspicious than I already am."

"But they're not suspicious of you, are they?"

"No, no, at least I don't think so, but don't worry, they still seem to love me. It just might start seeming suspicious if I keep hanging around the locker room after practice every day. Carl might think I have a crush on him."

"See what I mean?" I said, letting the waitress refill my mug. "We've got to act soon. What do you think I should tell your dad? Do I have any reason I can give for wanting to talk to him without letting him know you're playing detective?"

"Well, if you're really determined to speak to him, I think you already have an in, being you're still a key witness in Carmen's case, and she was your best friend. It's not out of line for you just to go to see him, if you want to." Seth's eyes were shining again, and I could see he was hatching a plan. "I mean, if he's the chief investigating officer in a case you are personally involved with, it's not out of line to want to simply talk to him. Come to think of it, you should be able to go to him and tell him anything you think might be pertinent to the case. We can make up some reasons for you to have your suspicions. Maybe you can just tell him that you have an uncomfortable feeling about some of the guys in the school, or maybe you can say you overheard something in the girls' room?"

"Yeah. I was thinking that might be how to play it. I wish we had something more concrete, though. I wish we could go to visit Jonny Freeman in the hospital."

"Have you heard anything more about him?"

"Not really. None of the girls I know were into him, he was such a predator, so no one I know goes to visit him in the hospital."

"He's still there?"

"Oh yeah, his burns and injuries were massive. They're still working on him. I think he's going to be in the hospital for a while yet. He's still getting skin grafts."

"How do you know so much?"

"My dad sometimes works at the UC Med Center, and he's been trying to keep me updated on Jonny's condition. I never really cared about how Jonny's recovery was going before, but now that I think he's involved, I've been asking. He told me something else that might be interesting. He told me that the coach and Skywalker are regular visitors."

"That's interesting about the coach, considering Jonny wasn't on the football team. You told me he was in track."

"That's right, but he was really tight with Skywalker, and since Luke's tight with the coach, maybe they're all good buddies."

"Hmmm. It is sounding more and more suspicious. Can you think of a good reason for you to pay a visit to Jonny at the hospital?"

"That's the hard part. Sadly, he doesn't know me from Adam. We've got to come up with an angle. Maybe there's a way I can use my connection to Carmen somehow. Or maybe I could just bring flowers and say they're from the student body?"

Seth chuckled. "No, the flowers would be pretty lame. It's a little late for that, but the Carmen connection might work. After all, since he said he saw Carmen in his car before the crash, maybe you could just be looking out for Carmen's ghost or something."

"Hey, maybe I could be writing a story for the school newspaper about sightings of Carmen's ghost!"

"But you don't work for the newspaper!"

"He doesn't know that!"

"You're right."

I took a long sip of my coffee and pondered for a few seconds.

"He doesn't actually know anything about me. And if he is the key to this whole thing, maybe he actually wants to say something about it. Maybe he's feeling remorse. Maybe I can get him to open up to me."

"Hey, slow down, you're getting ahead of yourself again. But the newspaper story sounds like your angle, and visiting him seems like a logical next step."

"What about my going to see your father, anyway? Just to get him on the same page?"

"You mean, to make sure he starts looking at the school?"

"Exactly. How's your hacking going? Have you seen anything in your dad's reports indicating that he's looking at the school yet?"

"Not really. They've only just received the personal security CCTV tapes for the Laurel Canyon area around Stephanie's house, and the video team is studying those now. And they're still looking out for similar crimes in the state and going over all the forensics again. But yes, so far, they have nada. So, you're probably right. It's about time for you to make a visit to the downtown LAPD administration building to stir things up a little. We should plan our visit to Jonny after that."

"Whoa there, does that mean you're planning to come with me to see Jonny?"

"Well, I could work for the newspaper too...."

"Wait a minute. Let's think about this realistically." And I put down my mug and looked at Seth, which made him put down his mug and look right back at me with his sincere ice blue eyes. "Remember what we've been discussing. We believe that these guys, Skywalker and maybe his friend Carl, pumped full of steroids and God knows what other drugs, kidnapped two girls and brutally beat, raped, and murdered them. Do you seriously think it's a good idea for you to be seen snooping around Jonny Freeman, the only real witness, if he might be involved?"

Seth sighed a deep sigh and nodded. "I see what you mean. You're right. It could be dangerous to be seen near Jonny Freeman right now—especially if he really turns out to be the third guy. Now that I think about it, maybe that's why the coach and Skywalker go visit him so often. Maybe they're just watching over him to make sure he doesn't talk."

"That's what I'm thinking. And that's why I think I should go to see your dad now—and not wait for any more evidence. Just to alert him to the possibilities. Okay?'

"Yeah. Definitely. Make that appointment."

I called Captain Greenberg's office from our booth at Pip's and made an appointment to see him downtown at the Homicide Division after school the next day. I thought he would probably have come to our house again, but I felt I should make more of an official statement. I hung up and looked across at Seth, who was watching me closely and grinning.

"What are you looking at?" I asked.

"Just imagining you at the LAPD. It's great. You'll do fine."

"I hope so." And I took out the notebook we used for our plans and jotted down some ideas for my meeting. I felt pretty good then. I felt like we were making the right moves. But even though I had warned Seth about the danger we could be getting ourselves into, fear went right out of my head. All I could concentrate on was being so close to finding Carmen's killers.

CHAPTER 22

THE CHAUFFEUR

I STOPPED by Angela's house that evening before I went home, like I did most days, to make sure she was okay. She had become noticeably edgy ever since Stephanie's murder, and James had wanted me to keep an eye on her. The police had reinterviewed her, just as they had me, along with everyone else in the neighborhood, which only served to rake up all the horror of the past year, but Angela remained amazingly strong and was still not drinking any alcohol, no matter how awful the circumstances became.

As soon as she opened the door and saw it was me, she exclaimed, "Oh, Lucy!" and took hold of my hand and dragged me into the kitchen. "Come in, come in! I've just made a fresh batch of iced tea." She seemed especially happy to see me. She looked lovely, her blonde hair in a shoulder-length bob, real pearls around her neck, and a robin's egg-blue sheath dress that brought out the blue of her eyes. I remembered it was Thursday, so she'd be going out to play bridge with my mom later that evening. She certainly did not appear to be on edge today.

"Now just sit down here at the table." And I sat down while she bustled about cheerfully and brought out the ice tea and poured it into tall, glistening glasses. Ever since James left, I'd made a point of staying in their kitchen when I visited, which was close to the front door and as far away from the living room or Carmen's bedroom as I could get. I didn't know why, but I no longer wanted to be in the parts of the house Carmen and I had made our own. I wasn't trying to forget her. I think I was just trying to let the wound scab over.

Angela was grinning her toothpaste-ad grin again as she carried the tray of tea and cookies and sat down across from me. "James is coming home for term break!" she announced. Well, no wonder she was suddenly so happy. He'd been away for nearly two months, but I knew he was worried about the latest events and how they would affect his mother.

"That's great! I can't wait to see him."

"And he wants to see you too. He told me you've still been keeping him up to date on the police investigation." Then she took a little sip of her iced tea and looked at me with unusual intensity. "James says you've discovered something new about Carmen's murder?"

Oh dear, I'd been keeping James in the loop about my investigation with Seth, but I hadn't told anyone else, not even Angela. I didn't want anything to compromise Seth—and certainly didn't want Seth's dad finding out about what we were up to.

"Uh, well, what exactly did James tell you?" I asked, looking down at the tray and pretending to be interested in her peanut butter cookies.

"Just that you had some new ideas about possible suspects. James thought your ideas made sense and that you were going to tell that nice Captain Greenberg about them." And she looked bright and hopeful, and I didn't know exactly what to answer.

"Well, yes... I have been thinking things through a bit, and I did make a connection with somebody that I think the police may have overlooked. It's something I don't think I ever mentioned to you."

"Oh? What was that?"

"It happened last year. Do you remember how we had this hysteria kind of thing happening at the school after Carmen was murdered? You know, where boys kept saying they saw her ghost?"

"Oh yes, but that was just a load of hogwash! You and I never believed any of that!"

"Well, something else did happen last year that I never told you about."

"What was that, dear?"

"There was this boy in our school, one of those rich-kid bad boys, you know the type: they think they can get away with anything and usually do? Anyway, you might have read about it in the paper at the time. It happened about a month after Carmen was murdered. This rich kid named Jonny Freeman had this terrible car wreck. He drove his car off the road into one of those canyons along Bellagio Road. He was nearly killed, and his injuries were so bad he's still in the hospital."

"I think I remember reading about it. And you think this boy had something to do with Carmen's murder?"

"Well, I know he did hang out with some of the other 'bad boys' on campus. I don't mean like criminals, just those kind of rich kids who rule the school just because they're good in sports and drive hot cars. It just seems to me now that some of them might have been involved, because when Stephanie was murdered, this Jonny Freeman was in the hospital, so he was out of the picture, which started me thinking. The police only found DNA from two killers in Stephanie's case, but the DNA turned out to be the same as two of the killers involved in Carmen's murder. Since there had been *three* guys in Carmen's case and now there were only *two*, it just made me think that Jonny Freeman might have been the third guy in Carmen's murder."

"A high school boy? How can that be?"

"I know it *sounds* far-fetched, but there is still one other detail that makes it even more possible. It's about this Jonny Freeman. When he woke up in the hospital after the wreck, he told the cops he saw Carmen sitting in the backseat of his car, and that's what made him lose control and drive off the road."

"You know that's just crazy talk."

"But maybe it was guilt that made him think he saw her ghost? And also, let me tell you, this guy was a real bastard, and a lot of the girls at school can testify to that. He treated girls really badly. I've overheard a lot of accusations against him in the girls' room."

"What sort of accusations?"

"Well, 'date rape' for one thing."

"But Carmen's murder was so brutal. Do you really think a high school boy could do something so horrible?"

"These aren't just boys, Angela. They're physically the size of men. They may be young in age, but they're still strong—and with the right leadership, they could be capable of anything. Remember, a lot of the boys at my school are old enough to be fighting in Iraq."

"So, do you have an idea of who the other two boys might be?"

"Well, I'm not totally sure, but I do have my suspicions, and I think I should tell Captain Greenberg. Just to see if he could maybe take a second look at the school."

Angela didn't look so happy now, but I didn't want to tell her everything I knew, like about the steroids and the cheerleaders and Coach Billy. I had purposely left out the whole football team connection, so I knew my story sounded pretty shaky. But I left it at that. She would be seeing my mom later, and I didn't want them discussing any of this. In fact, now I was afraid that I had already said too much.

"Please, Angela. Don't say anything to anybody. Not even to my mother. Please don't talk about this to anyone except James. Promise me?"

She reached out across the table and clasped my hand gently, looked into my eyes, and smiled her warm, Southern-style smile.

"Of course not, darling. You know I won't. I promise. Only with James."

And then she let go of my hand and changed the subject. "Goodness, James will be here next Friday! You'll come over for dinner on Saturday, won't you?"

"Of course. Thanks."

"I'll make you those Southern-fried tofu burgers you love!"

I went home for dinner and tried to study for a history exam, but all I could think about was what I would say to Captain Greenberg tomorrow. Explaining as much as I had to Angela made me feel less certain about my course of action, and even with my nightly Valium, it took me a long time to fall asleep. I couldn't stop worrying and planning, and when I finally fell asleep, I dreamed this crazy dream about Carmen.

Ever since the day I met Seth and we began our own investigation into Carmen's murder, I had stopped dreaming about her. I would still take a precautionary Valium before I went to bed each night, but I had been sleeping remarkably well lately. I thought this was because I was actually doing something for Carmen now, which not only made my life worth living again, but she didn't need to haunt my dreams anymore.

But that night, I dreamed I was standing in front of Carmen's house, looking toward her front door. It was already dark, and her porch light was on. As I watched, a gleaming black limousine came around the corner and pulled up across her driveway and waited. A few seconds later, the front door opened, and Carmen stepped out of the house, looking incredibly glamorous.

She was wearing her little black dress, only in my dream it was not so little anymore, for the hem came all the way down to her knees like a dress from the fifties, and she was wearing a white ermine stole around her shoulders and had long white gloves that went up the length of her slender arms. Her long hair was styled in a sexy fifties coiffeur, with a thick lock of lush brunette hair falling over one eye, just like Veronica Lake, a famous movie star we'd seen in old black-and-white films.

Suddenly, flashbulbs started going off, and I saw I was standing among a crowd of reporters and fifties-style paparazzi, politely hanging back and snapping Carmen's picture.

As she walked toward the car, the chauffeur stepped out of the limo, and I got a shock. It was Jonny Freeman! He looked very dapper in his uniform as he walked around the car and solicitously opened the passenger door for Carmen. She was facing the crowd now, and she beamed her wicked smile out to them as the flashbulbs went off once more. Then she slid gracefully into the backseat. I couldn't see if there was anyone else in the car, for the windows were tinted. Jonny came around the car and turned to wave at the crowd before stepping back inside the limo, and then he drove slowly down the hill.

Suddenly, I was watching the car from above as it made its way down Wilshire Boulevard. It was as if I were a camera in one of those traffic news helicopters. The limo was heading toward Santa Monica. A second later, I was transported somewhere else. I found myself in a familiar spot, leaning against a palm tree, looking out over neatly mowed lawns and gravestones scattered between the palm trees. Once again, I realized with a start, I was back at the Angelus Rosedale Cemetery. With my back to the tree, I had a good view of the limousine as it drove through the gates.

I was surrounded by reporters now, and I had to move forward with the rest of the crowd, following the limo as it headed up the drive. I knew we were going to Carmen's grave, and that was when I begin to feel fearful. I wanted to run away, but I was swept up in the crowd and could only move forward. In a few seconds, we were there. The limousine was parked alongside a freshly dug grave. There was a big pile of dark earth at the head of the grave. The whole scene was lit up by arc lamps, as if we were on a movie set.

Once again, Jonny Freeman, in his chauffeur getup, emerged from the limo and waved at the crowd. Then he walked around and opened Carmen's door. She stepped out, looking radiant, and the crowd of reporters cheered and took a thousand photos. Someone came up to her and put a huge bouquet of red roses into her arms, and she smiled again, that wicked smile I knew so well, and Jonny took her hand and led her right up to the edge of the grave.

I was filled with terror, and I wanted to shout to her, to warn her of something terrible that was about to happen, but I couldn't. I was paralyzed and could only watch. Then the two of them were standing at the edge of the grave, and Carmen threw the bouquet into the dark hole, and the crowd applauded. She gazed once more at the crowd, which was clapping and cheering, and she beamed her glorious smile at them and waved a gloved hand. And then Jonny pushed her over into the grave, and the lights went out.

I woke up in a sweat, my heart pounding. I had no idea what it actually meant, but it made me feel more certain than ever that I was on the right track with Jonny Freeman. I had to take another half a Valium, though, before I could fall back to sleep.

CHAPTER 23
DOWNTOWN

I HAD picked out my clothes carefully the night before, choosing what I thought would make a good impression on the LAPD when I made my appearance there later in the day. I felt overdressed and conspicuous in my power-red top and black jeans when I arrived at school the next morning, but Seth didn't seem to notice anything different about me, and after lunch we went over and over my statement until I began to relax. I thought I knew exactly what I was going to say to Seth's dad, but when I hopped on the Santa Monica Freeway after school and headed for the downtown LAPD administration building, my stomach twisted, and my head began to buzz, and I knew I would forget everything.

I made it to the police admin parking lot by three thirty and found my way to the LAPD building, which turned out to be an imposing multistory construction with a not-surprisingly large police presence outside the entrance. I hadn't been downtown in a long while, and I was surprised at how clean and modern everything looked. Feeling much too young, I walked up the steps as gracefully as possible.

As soon as I entered through the automatic doors, I was greeted by the building's security team, had my handbag searched and scanned, and had to show them my ID.

Once I had cleared that station and made my way to reception, a uniformed policewoman looked me over, and after studying my ID again, asked me what my business was at police headquarters that day. When I told her I had an appointment with Captain Greenberg, she looked me up and down again with an expression verging on respect and asked a nice-looking black officer to escort me to the captain's office. This was fortunate, as the building turned out to be massive and had very poor signage. I would never have found my way there myself.

The officer was very friendly and told me his name was Ron and proceeded to guide me through a maze of corridors and up and down several elevators, using his passkey at every barrier until I was completely baffled.

"So what are you doing over at homicide today, miss?" he asked, making conversation.

"I just need to speak with Captain Greenberg about one of the cases he's working on."

"Are you a friend of that high school girl who's just been murdered?"

"Not really. I go to the same school, though."

We finally turned down a hall where a large sign proclaimed the Robbery Homicide Division, and then down another hall to a door with a smoky glass window and a sign reading HSS—Homicide Special Section. Ron pressed a little button outside the door, and someone inside buzzed us in.

This room turned out to be a spacious but typically antiseptic room with a big counter across the middle separating the waiting area from the working area, not unlike the reception room in our own high school admin building. There were loads of desks behind the counter with lots of haggard-looking people, some in uniforms, but many in street clothes, busily answering telephones, reading files, and filling out forms.

Ron led me to the counter and called to an attractive Hispanic woman bending over the shoulder of a guy on a phone at a desk nearby. "Hey, Rosie, this young lady has an appointment with the new captain."

She looked up and smiled at me in a way that put me immediately at ease. Then she walked up to the counter and opened what looked like an appointment book. She was casually dressed in a charcoal-gray pantsuit with a white blouse open at the throat, revealing a tiny gold cross shining against her honey-brown skin. If she was a policewoman, she was the prettiest one I had ever seen outside of a television show. Her shoulder-length dark hair framed a small, fine-boned face, and she wore just enough makeup to accentuate her almond-shaped eyes and full lips.

"Ah, you must be Lucy?" she asked, looking up at me and smiling again. "Just take a seat, and I'll tell the captain you're here." She turned around and walked to a door I hadn't noticed, over on the side. She opened the door and slipped in, quickly shutting the door behind her.

I picked out a plastic chair near a table with magazines and sat down.

"I'll just leave you in Rosie's fine hands, then, miss. You have a good day now." And Ron left me there, leafing through a five-year-old copy of *Reader's Digest*. But Rosie was only gone a minute or two, and when she returned, she was followed by Seth's dad, Captain Greenberg himself.

He was smiling at me, and he put out his hand for me to shake, like an adult. "Hello, Lucy. Nice to see you again."

I stood up and shook his hand and mumbled some kind of greeting while he turned to Rosie. "Why don't you get us some coffee, Rosie. You'd like that, wouldn't you, Lucy? Milk and sugar?"

"Black will be fine, sir," I answered. "Thank you."

"Well, just follow me into my office. You'll have one up on Seth. He's never seen the inside of the LAPD." He turned, and I followed him through the break in the counter, then through that same door to the side of the reception area.

It opened onto another surprisingly large room, but this one had a gigantic desk with stacks of file folders piled on top. There were bookshelves covering every wall from floor to ceiling, and I could see they were absolutely stuffed with heavy books, most of them looking like law or some other kind of reference book. There were four tall filing cabinets also topped with stacks of files, a large whiteboard on a stand facing out from one of the corners, and several miscellaneous chairs for visitors. Behind the desk, the window took up most of the back wall. The venetian blind was half-open, giving a pretty good view of downtown LA, but the office chair had its back to the window, and it looked like whomever sat there had plenty inside the room to occupy their attention.

"I'll just move one of these chairs a bit closer," he said, as he slid a not-too-shabby leather visitor's chair right up to the desk. "Please, sit down."

I sat, while Captain Greenberg took his place behind the big desk. He looked across at me for a second, but didn't say anything. Then he started leafing through a file that was right in front of him. I wondered, for a second, how I was supposed to begin, but just then, Rosie came back into the room carrying a tray with coffee and donuts. Captain Greenberg hastily moved some files out of the way to make just room enough for Rosie to set down the tray.

"There you are. We had some fresh donuts in the lounge. I thought you might like one." And she looked over at me and cracked another smile. Her teeth were shockingly white. She made me think she was offering me an after-school snack, and I suddenly felt very young.

"Thank you, Rosie," the captain said, choosing a fat jelly donut and taking a big bite out of it, just the way Seth would have done, picking up a napkin in his other hand to wipe away the sugar from his face and fingers. "Help yourself, Lucy. Don't be shy."

I was too nervous to be hungry, so I lifted a mug of coffee and said, "Thank you, I'm just happy to have coffee right now."

"If you don't mind, I'm going to finish reading this file for a minute. It just came in. Then I'll be ready to talk to you."

He continued to munch on his donut while leafing through the file, stopping every now and then to look back over something and make notes on a pad nearby. Then he finished his donut, wiped his mouth with the napkin, closed the file, and looked over at me.

"I know you are understandably interested in both of these murder cases, but particularly your friend Carmen's case, and I know you've been talking to Seth about it." He was looking at me kindly, so I just sat there and nodded, not knowing quite where he was headed.

"I want you to know that that's all right. You can talk to my son about the case, but I also want you to understand that *I* am not going to talk to Seth about these cases myself. I also do not want you to speak to him about anything we discuss in this office. He's not involved, and he shouldn't be involved. But I think you have the right to know what we've found out so far and where we are headed in our investigation."

I caught my breath. Was he really going to be frank with me? "Thank you" was all I said.

"So, let me tell you a few things we know to be true." He put down his coffee mug. "I told you the last time we met that we would be looking out for similar crimes either here in California or out of state, crimes with the same MO or with a similar level of brutality." He stopped suddenly, as if he had just remembered something. "Are you all right with me talking to you like this? I'm not making you uncomfortable, am I?"

"No, I'm fine. Please go ahead."

"Well, first of all, we've looked for similar crimes—and we've been in contact with the FBI profile team on this also. We've concluded that, although there have been other similarly brutal murders of women, some with nearly as much savagery as these two murders, the crimes we have here are unusual. This is because crimes of this nature almost always prove to be the work of one perpetrator. Occasionally, we'll come across a helper, or what we call 'a facilitator,' who might be a friend or sometimes even a wife. These people are often used to lure the victims into a vehicle or a home, but these helpers don't usually take part in the actual rapes or murders. It just doesn't happen. Crimes of this sort are almost always the work of one individual. But here, we have a case where there are three perpetrators involved. We almost never see that except in war crimes.

"Then there's the fact that now we have two similar crimes committed by two of the same perpetrators. Usually, when we discover two crimes by the same perpetrator, we're talking about a serial killer. And again, when we talk about serial killers, they are almost always the work of one individual, although, once again, sometimes they will have a facilitator. Still, crimes like these just don't exist with three perpetrators."

"But there were only two perpetrators in Stephanie's case," I chimed in.

"Yes, you're right. In other crimes, like robberies, which are often performed by gangs or groups of perpetrators, it is not unusual for the MO to change, for one or two of the guys to drop out, whatever, because it doesn't always have to be the same group of guys. Maybe some are now in prison, maybe they've moved away, but it's not important for the crime.

"But in murders this brutal, it would be almost impossible for one of the participants to just stop, to tell the others 'I quit.' It would be far too dangerous for the other two. Even if one of them did have a change of heart, even if he felt remorse, whatever the case might be, the other two couldn't let him off the hook. They would be afraid that this one might go to the police. In other words, he would become a liability. What I am saying is that it would be completely out of character for this third person to remain alive after crimes like these."

All the time he was talking, Captain Greenberg hardly looked at me. He just kept looking down at his files or at his mug of coffee. He had picked out another donut, this time a cinnamon roll, and he munched on it between sentences. When he lifted his eyes to mine, he looked serious, and he made no attempt to smile.

"So, one of the lines we are pursuing is a search for this third guy."

I didn't say anything then and waited for him to go on, but I was cheering inside.

"Another line we are pursuing is the vehicle. We know they used the same vehicle in both crimes. We've been looking over the videotapes from all the CCTV cameras near any of the scenes, either where the girls were picked up or where their bodies were found."

I caught my breath. Even though we were talking about Carmen's murder, hearing the word "body" in reference to Carmen always brought back the horror of those photos I had seen from forensics, the photos Captain Greenberg had no idea I had seen.

"We've just finished studying the tapes from the gas station in Malibu, on the corner near where Carmen's body was found. Now our team is cross-referencing license plates from the other crime scenes. And we've also taken another look at the upholstery fibers found in the first investigation to make certain they were the same as the new ones picked up in the second forensics search, and we can definitely conclude that they are." He looked down at that last file he had been looking at before continuing, "This time, my crew noted that the color was more significant than was first thought, because although the upholstery fabric is generic in all high-end SUVs, the color will only match a certain number of vehicle models for each make because of the color coordination with the exterior paint choice." He looked over at me again and interrupted his line of thought.

"I know this probably sounds really boring, but it can prove very helpful, because we now know that the fabric fibers are from an upholstery color called 'Midnight Charcoal,' which was only installed in vehicles manufactured by Mercedes, Porsche, or the General Motors' Hummer and of those, they had to match the exterior paints. Fortunately for us, these exterior paints came in only two colors, 'Onyx Black' or 'Charcoal.' This will definitely narrow the field."

Now he was looking at me with almost a gleam in his eye. "So you see, Lucy. This all brings me to the last line of investigation that we've been pursuing. Do you want another cup of coffee?" he asked suddenly, apropos of nothing except maybe his own empty cup, but by now I was too speechless to do anything but nod my head.

He pushed his chair back and got up and walked out of the office, evidently in pursuit of Rosie. I guess the intercom wasn't working, or maybe he just needed to stretch those long legs of his. Anyway, he returned a few minutes later.

"Rosie will be back in a minute with the coffee," he said as he sat down again. He didn't say anything for a while and just sat there with his elbows on his desk, resting his chin against his fist, staring at the remaining donuts. Then he looked up and continued without cracking a smile.

"I know you've been impatient with us for constantly asking if the girls knew their attackers, and you insist that neither girl did, and at any rate, they would never have willingly gotten into a vehicle driven by anyone, whether they knew them or not. Well, that's all well and good, but we have come down to the bottom line here, and with what we know, we are pretty certain that the girls *did* know their attackers. We are pretty certain that these were local guys, local meaning from their part of Los Angeles—and judging by the cost of the vehicle, these were probably guys going to the same local high school." And he stopped and looked at me again. "That means your high school, Lucy. And Seth's high school."

The way he was looking at me made me think he might actually be aware that Seth and I were undertaking our own clandestine investigation. But before I could get too uncomfortable, Rosie opened the door and walked in holding a pot of fresh coffee, and we sat there in silence while she refilled our cups.

When she left, Captain Greenberg took a long sip from his mug and continued. "What I mean to say is that we are fairly certain that there are some very brutal students walking among you, and I want you two to watch out for each other. That buddy system they encourage you to participate in. That's a smart idea. We're not ready to go to the school officially with our suspicions, so we can't do anything publicly yet, so please, Lucy, just be careful." I didn't know what to say, so I took another sip of coffee and nodded.

"The school is aware that we have extended our investigation to include the staff as well as the student body, and they are helping us with this. We have asked the administration to provide us with all the names of students fifteen years of age and over, meaning those who can drive and might own a car, as well as all the staff, the teachers, and substitute teachers who worked at the school during both years the girls were murdered.

"We'll run the list through DMV to get all the vehicles registered to these students and teachers, as well as the vehicles registered to the parents of the students. Once we've cross-referenced all this information with what we have from the CCTV tapes, we'll be that much closer to catching them. I just wanted you to know this—that we are closing in."

"I'm amazed that you've made so much progress," I said, putting my mug down on the desk.

Finally, he leaned forward again, and asked, "So what have you come here to tell me today?"

I stared down into my coffee mug, my mind a blur with all this new information I'd just heard. Then I decided to go ahead and speak.

"I just came to tell you that I've been thinking along those same lines. That it must be guys connected to our school somehow. Only, because I'm actually at the school, I might have heard some other stuff that could have a bearing on all this."

He perked up and swiveled around in his chair. "Oh, what have you heard?"

"Well, sometimes when I'm in the girls' restroom, I hear all kinds of things that the girls wouldn't tell me themselves, when they think they're alone with their friends. And one of the things I've heard is that the coach of the football team has been feeding the team steroids."

"But what has this got to do with these murders?"

"Well, I'm sure you've heard about ''roid rage,' and I don't know if you're aware of this, but our school has one of the worst records for unsportsmanlike conduct on the field. I mean, they play rough, really rough!"

"Okay, I see where you're going. That's interesting. And you say the coach is involved? What did you say the coach's name was?"

"Billy Boehm." And I spelled it for him. "He just came to our school a little over a year ago from some junior college in the Midwest."

"All right, we'll look into him. Quietly. We don't want to raise any flags at the school yet. Anything else you've noticed?"

"The coach seems to be way too buddy-buddy with some of the players. Luke Ritter, for one, that's the quarterback, and Carl Brandt. I don't know what position he plays. Maybe a running back."

"Okay." And he wrote those names down also.

"And I think I know who the third guy is."

He stopped writing and turned to me with a look of total surprise.

CHAPTER 24
MY CLEVER PLAN

ONCE I started talking, it was easy to keep going, and I told the captain the entire Jonny Freeman saga. Naturally, none of his predecessors on the force would have attached any significance to a teenage car wreck or would have tied it to Carmen's murder in any way. But Captain Greenberg was immediately engaged; I could see him working through the possibilities in his mind as he listened. I even told him about the instant urban mythology that had sprouted up after Carmen's murder.

I told him everything, from Jonny's history of rapes, including my firsthand experience with Wendy's escape from Mulholland Drive, up to Jonny's flaming crash and him insisting he saw Carmen's ghost in the backseat of his car before he ran off the road.

"This is really interesting, Lucy," Captain Greenberg said at the end of my story. He had been leaning forward over the desk, watching my face and listening closely the entire time, except when he paused to jot something down on his pad. "This boy's thinking that he saw Carmen's ghost could definitely be a sign of his guilty conscience. You could be right about him having hallucinations because of it, and this hysteria that you noted taking place around the boys' locker room, that's also very interesting and ties in with what you've been telling me about the football coach. Maybe someone else is suffering from a guilty conscience."

He rocked back in his chair and fiddled with a pencil, turning it over and over between his two hands as he thought about my story. Then he stopped fiddling with the pencil and stared past me at the bookshelves before he continued.

"Now, we have a difficult situation here in that our getting a warrant to take this boy's DNA won't be easy without any hard evidence—which is exactly why we need his DNA. If we make an official visit to the hospital, it might arouse the suspicions of his two partners, especially at this late date. We have to think this through and proceed with caution."

"Well, sir," I piped up, a sudden thought crossing my mind. "I had kind of been planning to go by and visit him—I was going to tell him that I was writing a story about Carmen's ghost for the school paper, *The Wildcat*."

He turned in his chair and looked at me sternly. "I don't think you should go anywhere near that hospital, Lucy."

"But, sir, if it could help, I could wear a wire!"

His expression changed then, and I could see he was thinking about the possibilities, but he didn't dismiss the idea out of hand. "You know we couldn't let you do that, but there may be other options." He stared at his telephone for a moment, then looked back at me with almost a smile on his face. "You don't think he would be suspicious if you visited him? Since you say you don't really know him at all?"

"Well, from what I've been told, he doesn't get many visitors. He's still really bad off, physically. I don't think he's going to be a threat to me, and like you say, with his guilty conscience, maybe he'll want to talk to someone—and I can be that someone."

Captain Greenberg sat up straight then and reached for one of the phones he'd been staring at a moment ago, then hesitated, thinking better of it. "Do you have to be anywhere now?" he asked, replacing the receiver. "Can you stay here a while longer?"

"No problem."

"Okay. Do me a favor and go back into the waiting room. Let me talk to my team and the DA. We'll see what our options are."

"Okay," I answered, getting up and letting myself out while he started punching numbers into the phone and thinking to myself, *Oh wow, this is way better than I expected.* I couldn't wait to tell Seth.

When I got back into the waiting room, the visitor's section was still empty. I said hi to Rosie to let her know I was there and sat down in my corner with the old magazines. It was a funny sort of office, I guess because it was HSS—a special section for special crimes, serial killers and the like. They had this big waiting room, but no one was waiting. Officers were walking in and out carrying files, showing things to Rosie at reception, and walking back behind the counter to talk with other detectives. I guess it was a detective's showcase, not really for the public.

"Would you like something a little more exciting to read?" Rosie asked. She had seen me sit down and pick up that old copy of *Reader's*

Digest. She was holding a copy of something called *New Criminologist* in her hand, and she was offering it to me.

"Thank you," I said, and took it. It made for some riveting reading while I waited, which was good, as I felt as though I was sitting on pins and needles and had to fight the impulse to text Seth.

While I sat there, I could see Rosie talking to several detectives, and as I watched, they each grabbed files off their desks and headed through the door to Captain Greenberg's office. Then an elegantly dressed woman carrying a sheaf of papers under her arm was buzzed in to the waiting room. She walked right up to Rosie, but I couldn't hear what she was saying to her; then she followed Rosie through the same door into Captain Greenberg's office, and I suspected she must be an assistant DA.

Fifteen minutes later, when I was deep into an article on digital forensics, Rosie tapped me on the shoulder. "The captain would like to see you again, Lucy."

"Okay." I handed her back the magazine and followed her through the door into Captain Greenberg's office. The DA lady was perched on my seat, but there was another chair just behind it, and Rosie pulled it closer to the desk for me and asked everyone if they'd like some more coffee. There were still two donuts on the plate, and now I was hungry, so I said yes, please, and helped myself to a maple bar.

"Thank you for waiting outside, Lucy," said the captain. "And now I'd like you to meet Miss Trujillo. She's an assistant district attorney, and she's given us some helpful advice."

Miss Trujillo was watching me trying to nibble gracefully at my maple bar, but she had a benign smile on her face, even though her figure told me she had probably never devoured so much as a donut crumb in her life. It was delicious, but I stopped eating and set it down on top of a napkin and said hello to her.

"The captain tells me that you have volunteered to wear a wire in order to vet a potential witness and possible suspect," she told me, which sounded like an awfully grand plan. I nodded, and she continued.

"I've told the captain that this will not be necessary—and would probably be an actionable offence, as you are both underage and a civilian."

I couldn't hide my disappointment at these words, but she kept talking. "However, if you wish to visit this person without wearing a wire, and he admits to you that he is involved with the murder of your friend, then your testimony, while not admissible in court except as hearsay, would be enough to get us the warrant to extract the suspect's DNA."

"Any statements he makes to you can also be repeated in court, but only as evidence that he made such a statement, not that we believe it to be the truth. But that's getting ahead of ourselves. Right now, I think the captain would like to get ahold of a sample of this person's DNA for comparison, and any information you can get that will enable us to proceed to a warrant will be very valuable." And she smiled, a tight, restrained, and official smile, but still a smile.

"I'd like to help. Anything I can do that will help is just fine with me, really."

"All right, then." And Miss Trujillo stood up, all five feet nine inches of educated elegance. She shook hands with the captain, who had risen also. "You've had my advice now. I can see nothing wrong if our witness wants to visit a fellow student in the hospital." Then she turned to me and smiled her elegant assistant-DA smile.

"Thank you, Lucy. I hope to be seeing you again soon." And she glided out of the room while we all stood around looking far less elegant.

"Right, then," said Captain Greenberg, looking over at me. "You've probably had a long enough day today. I suggest you go home and think about all this, and if you decide to pay this Jonny Freeman a visit, that would be terrific, but give me a call first. Do you still have my card with my direct line on it?"

"Actually, no, I seem to have lost it."

He took one out of a cardholder on his desk and handed it to me. "You know that we would be really grateful if you did make that visit. You do understand that, don't you?"

I nodded and tucked the card safely away in the back pocket of my jeans.

"But call me *first* before you go. All right? *Don't* pay that visit without calling me first. You said he was at the USC Burn Center? That's quite a ways away from where you live, but it's just off the I-10, and traffic might not be so heavy this weekend, if you're thinking of going soon."

"Actually, I was. I was thinking of going tomorrow," I said. "It's Saturday, and I thought, the sooner the better. I just hope he's willing to talk to me. Or that something will come out of it. I don't suppose you want me to take anything belonging to him away with me, like a hairbrush or toothbrush?" I'd seen detectives doing this on TV shows to sneak out DNA specimens.

"As much as we would love to have either of those objects, without a warrant and proof of the chain of evidence, we'd only shoot ourselves in the foot if we made it to trial. We'll just proceed by the book for now."

"Okay," I said.

"Thank you again for coming in, Lucy. And you won't be talking about any of this to Seth, will you?"

"Oh no, sir. No." And I started walking toward the door. "I guess I had better be going now."

"At least rush hour is over," he said, looking at his watch. And I glanced at mine. Wow, it was six thirty already. "Drive carefully, Lucy."

"Good-bye," I called as I slipped through the door and up to the counter, where Rosie was ticking items off on a clipboard.

"Thanks for the magazine, Rosie. It was really interesting," I said to her, and I was just about to leave the office when I remembered I had no idea how to get out of there and find the entrance to the building again.

"Wait right there, girl," she told me. "Civilians aren't allowed to walk around here without an escort." She flashed her warm smile at a young officer who had just delivered a file to the in-box on her counter. "Tim here will escort you out, won't you, Tim?"

CHAPTER 25
HERE'S JONNY

I CALLED Seth from my car even before I left the parking garage. I told him everything that had happened in the meeting, everything his dad told me, and everything I had said to his dad, including the promise I had made not to tell Seth anything about our meeting.

"Wow, that's great! My dad's not such a bad detective after all. He's put together more than we could tell from reading his case notes. I guess he keeps a lot of this stuff in his head. It's good to know he's on the ball in case it starts getting tense in the locker room. At least I'll know he's behind me, even though he'd be angry as hell if he knew what I've been doing. So, should I drive you over to see Jonny tomorrow?"

"Oh no," I answered. "Definitely not! I think you should stay as far away from that hospital as possible. Your dad might have a surveillance team there or something. And also, don't forget that the coach and Skywalker have been visiting Jonny pretty regularly, and you could really get caught out."

"But you're not going there alone, are you?"

"Actually, that's what I had planned, but now that you mention it, maybe it would be good to have someone with me, someone to act as lookout. I think I'll call Wendy and see if she's free. I need to talk to her about the cheerleaders anyway, and we can do that on the ride to the hospital. And you know what else I think?"

"No, what?"

"I think I should tell Wendy about what we're doing."

"You really think that's wise? You'll be blowing my cover!"

"But I think she can really help us. Wendy's not actually involved with any of those people. She might not be the sharpest knife in the drawer, but she's got good instincts—and she hates the social order just as much as we do. She's just better placed in it, which is a good thing for us because we can use whatever she can dig up. Also, I know she really likes me, and I believe that she'll do just about anything I ask her to."

"Well, that's something. Okay. If you're cool with it, I'm cool with it. But you have to be careful. Now that we know we're probably on the right track, we all could be in real danger, I mean, like, dangerous danger. Do you know what I mean? We don't want Wendy to get hurt either!"

I waited until I got home safely and had dinner with the family before I telephoned Wendy. She was home on a Friday night because she wasn't dating anyone. Actually, I never saw Wendy with anyone at all, except her choreographer and her casual girlfriends from school—and I only saw them on campus.

Anyway, it was late when we finished dinner, and even though she lived only five houses down the street, I didn't dare walk down there alone, and I didn't want to ask Constanza to escort me, so I called Wendy on my cell and talked to her from my bedroom. I told her everything from the start, from when I first met Seth to my visit with Seth's dad today.

"Wow! I can't believe it!" she exclaimed. "But it makes sense. It must all have to do with that creepy coach. I've been having this sick feeling that he's been abusing the girls on the cheerleading squad all this time, and that's why they're all acting weird. Christ, and that Jonny Freeman too. It all makes sense."

So even Wendy could see it. Of course, she had firsthand knowledge of Jonny Freeman's bad attitude toward women, so that probably helped. Wendy said she would come to the hospital with me and act as my lookout. So we made plans to meet up right after lunch on Saturday.

I called Seth's dad the next morning after breakfast to tell him I was definitely going and what time I would be at the hospital. "Be careful, Lucy. Don't ask anything too obvious. Don't make yourself vulnerable. Promise?"

"Yes, I promise. I'll just ask my school paper questions and hope he *wants* to open up to me."

"Good. That's great. Good luck, then, and don't forget to call me as soon as you get home. Okay?"

"Right, chief," I said, half joking, and then, at just after 1:00 p.m., I picked Wendy up at her house, and off we went to the USC Burn Unit in deepest downtown LA. We had already decided that, after we got parked up, we would scope out the hospital, locate the cafeteria, have a cup of coffee, and then have Wendy wait there while I visited Jonny. She had brought her Kindle to read while she waited, so she was all set. She was pretty excited to be part of Seth's and my investigation, and just as I thought, she was just terrifically pleased to be doing something with me besides algebra.

I had already downloaded a map to the burn unit. USC had a huge medical center, so I wanted to be prepared. It took us over an hour to drive there, but Wendy kept up a string of questions about what Seth and I were doing, and we were talking so much that before I knew it, I was turning my car into the parking lot and looking for a space.

We made our way to the hospital entrance, where we were greeted by one of those pretty young candy stripers who was about our age, all smiles and good teeth, so to make her happy and our lives easier, we asked her where the cafeteria was. She gave us directions, and we found it without too much trouble by following a green stripe she showed us that was painted on the floor. It took us down the stairs and around a bend until we found the cafeteria overlooking the back of the hospital, with a broad sunny terrace where the nurses and interns could take their lunch out in the sun.

We chose a table inside, and Wendy sat with her back to the window, facing the entrance to the cafeteria. I didn't know why we chose the cafeteria as our lookout point. It probably would have been sensible to wait in the entrance lobby of the hospital where we could keep our eyes on anyone entering the building, but that seemed so uncomfortable and too conspicuous. I didn't really think I needed a lookout, anyway, but it was nice to have the company. I bought the coffees for Wendy and me, and I sat down just long enough to realize the coffee tasted like crap, and I should have ordered a cappuccino. Then we synchronized our cell phones, and I left, making my way to the elevators that would take me to the fourth floor.

The burn unit *was* a big deal. State of the art and one of the best in the country, so there were lots of signs pointing the way, and I had no trouble finding it, as it took up more than half of the fourth floor. On the way up, I managed to get a good look at myself in the elevator mirror and decided to stop off at a restroom as soon as I got off to straighten myself out a bit. Fortunately, there was one right alongside the elevator, so I made good use of it and emerged looking like what I imagined a high school girl who worked on the school newspaper should look.

I made my way to the unit's reception desk and asked where Jonny's room was. They seemed surprised to see me, and I remembered that Jonny didn't get many visitors, so I just smiled and said I was from the school newspaper. One of the nurses escorted me down the hall, through what looked like the patients' lounge, where several patients sat wrapped in bandages that made them look like mummies. They were attached to IV trolleys and seemed to be watching sports TV. Nobody looked very happy. I steeled myself for my meeting with Jonny. A little farther down the hall, we came to what must have been his room because the nurse knocked on the door.

"Jonny? You have a visitor."

There was something that sounded like a moan coming from behind the door, so the nurse opened it a crack and peeked her head around. "Oh, hi, Jonny. Hope I'm not disturbing you. Are you all right?"

I heard another moaning kind of sound and wondered what the hell I had gotten myself into, but the nurse kept on as if everything was perfectly normal. "There's a girl from your school here to see you. Can I bring her in?"

It had never occurred to me that he could refuse to see me, but then, I hadn't known just how bad off he was.

"It's all right. You can go in," she said to me, and she held the door open for me to slip past her.

The first thing I saw upon entering was some festive-looking flowers in a big vase on the nightstand, and the thought flashed through my mind that I should have brought some flowers with me, and then I looked over at the bed and there he was.

He was a shock to see. He seemed to be completely wrapped up in bandages like the invisible man, including his face. He was looking in my direction but with only one eye, because the other was still half-shut from the burn scars. His hands were wrapped up too, and he still had an IV feed. And this was seven months since his accident! I was so stunned I just started rambling, saying anything plausible that came into my head to explain my being there.

"Hello, Jonny," I began. "You don't know me, but my name is Lucy and, uh, I'm majoring in journalism and we, umm, are doing a story for *The Wildcat*, that's the school newspaper. Anyway, we're doing a story about the school being haunted and, uh, we thought we should ask about your seeing Carmen's ghost in your car the night of your accident. Do you mind talking about it?"

As I talked, Jonny just collapsed back against his pillows and closed his one good eye, and I thought, well, that's that. But then he must have pressed a button that raised the top end of the bed higher so he could be in a sitting position without straining. He turned his head slowly to look at me, a movement that looked terribly painful, but he still didn't say anything.

I had taken a notepad out of my handbag in the restroom to make me look very efficient, but now I started stuffing it back in my bag.

"Look, if this is a bad time, I'll just come back...."

He shook his head with what looked like great effort, and then he finally said something. His voice was so soft and so low I could hardly make out the words. "It hurts to talk" was what I figured he said.

"Look, I'll just come back another time." And I made as if to leave.

"No. Please stay." He said this slightly louder, but still in his soft, hoarse voice. And he leaned back after he said this as if it had taken all his strength to utter those few words, and closed his eye again. After a few moments, he turned his head toward me and kind of nodded toward the chair by his bed. "Please sit down."

He was so terrible to look at, it made me afraid to come close to him, but I remembered my mission, and I said thank you and sat down primly on the seat next to his bed. I was so close to him I could see the layers of bandages and all the other tubes and bags that were attached to him and to his bed. He was obviously in really bad shape.

He looked at me again with his one good eye, which fortunately was his right eye, so it was closest to me, and he didn't have to turn his head too far. "I think I remember seeing you around campus," he said, and even under the bandages, I could see his face contort in pain when he talked for longer than a few syllables. "Sorry," he went on, "it hurts to talk. It hurts to do anything."

And he leaned back against his pillows again.

I thought maybe he had passed out, but then he suddenly spoke again. "I saw her, all right," he said, looking up at the ceiling. "She's damned me to hell."

"What do you mean?" I asked, all innocence.

"I deserved this. I know I deserved this, but you've got no idea how bad it feels." His voice was louder now, and I could see him straining to look at me. "I saw her ghost, all right, and now I'm in hell."

"Did she say anything to you?" I asked, trying to keep my voice neutral.

"She didn't need to. She didn't need to say anything." He shook his head stiffly, as if his neck were in a cast. "Now my life is over. It's all over. I just want to die now, but they won't let me."

This was a lot heavier than even I had expected it would be. The boy was so obviously in severe distress. He really did look like he was suffering the torments of hell. He might have been responsible for the cruel and brutal attack on Carmen, but now I couldn't stop myself from feeling sorry for him.

"Oh, don't say that. Please don't say that," I said, like any girl would. "I'm sure things will get better for you. You'll get better. Everything will be all right," I said, using all the lies everyone always uses, but he wasn't having any of it.

"No, you don't understand," he groaned out these words. "My life is really over. I've ruined it, and now all I can feel is pain. I'm in so much pain, you can't imagine. I feel like I'm in hell now. Nothing can save me. It's over. It's all over for me."

He kept shaking his head back and forth, even though I could see it hurt like hell to do it. I wondered if he was feeling terrible pain physically or if he was feeling the terrible anguish of remorse. He finally stopped writhing around and turned his head away from me and started to cry. I could tell it really hurt him to cry, because he moaned in pain between his sobs, and I felt truly awful. But at the same time, I felt as if I was close to an answer.

That's when I got the text from Wendy. *The coach is here! Luke and the coach just walked into the cafeteria. They're getting some sandwiches!*

I tried to text back as unobtrusively as possible while Jonny moaned with his back to me. "I remember who you are," he said suddenly.

I was startled, but I texted Wendy back quickly, *Are they coming up here?*

"You're Carmen's friend," Jonny moaned. "I'm so sorry. So terribly sorry." He began sobbing even louder, and I couldn't ask him what he was sorry about. Was it a confession? Could I use it in court?

Wendy texted back, *I think you should get out of there now—and I'll meet you at the car.*

Shit. You're right, I texted back.

Jonny was sobbing softer now, almost as if he was falling asleep. I stood up. "Jonny?" I asked quietly.

"It's all right. Please go away now. Just leave me alone."

"I'm sorry, Jonny. I'm really sorry. I hope you feel better." At that moment, I meant it. If it was possible, and I wasn't sure it was, he looked as if he had suffered enough.

I stuffed my notepad into my handbag and slipped out the door as silently as I could and ran down the hall and through the patients' lounge and called good-bye to the nurses at the reception desk as I ran past on my way to the elevator. There were two elevators, and happily for me, the left-hand one had its doors open, ready to go down, but just as I made to step inside, the other elevator arrived, and its doors opened, and the coach and Luke stepped out into the hall. I quickly looked down at my shoes and rushed into the other elevator and pressed the ground floor button. I didn't know if they actually saw me, and I didn't know if they would have recognized me if they *had* seen me.

All I know is what happened later.

CHAPTER 26
BYE-BYE JONNY

WENDY WAS waiting for me by the car. I had forgotten to give her my keys, but I was so stunned after my meeting with Jonny and so terrified that Luke and the coach might have seen me that I ran the entire length of the hospital and all the way to the parking lot. I was so happy to see her there that I gave her a sweaty hug and a grateful thank you before unlocking the car. Then we climbed in and scooted out of there and onto the I-10 in record time.

I talked the whole way about how shocking Jonny looked and how surreal my meeting with him had been. I was pretty shaken by the experience and still didn't know what to make of it. His misery was so real. It was hard to believe he could have ever inflicted the kind of suffering Carmen had endured. But in my heart, I felt it was true and that he really was sorry and possibly felt guilty and distressed enough to want to tell the DA. Then I began to fret about seeing the coach and Luke again. I just hoped to hell they hadn't recognized me.

When I dropped Wendy off at her house, we made plans to hang out at her house the next day. I still wanted to ask her about the cheerleaders. But right then I needed to call Seth's dad like I had promised, and I needed to call Seth later too.

I called Seth's dad as soon as I got home. Whatever he was doing on that Saturday evening, he stopped as soon as he heard my voice. I could hear a television in the background and then him walking into another room and closing the door, so I guess he was home and had gone into his study to speak to me in private.

"Hello, Lucy, how did it go today?" he asked casually, as if he were asking me about a baseball game or a science exam.

"Well, I think it went well, but it was much harder than I thought it would be." And for some reason, I didn't know why, I just started crying.

"Lucy, are you all right? Did anything happen to you? Should I send somebody over?"

"No, no," I sobbed, grabbing a wad of Kleenex from the coffee table, "it's just that he's in really bad shape. Jonny, I mean. He's really fucked up bad. He can hardly speak, and he's still covered up in bandages. He's in a lot of pain."

"Could you talk to him at all?"

"Well, I didn't really get a chance to talk much. He was in such terrible pain, and he was crying and moaning the whole time. It was terrible."

"I'm so sorry, Lucy. That must have been awful for you."

I stopped crying then. I needed to tell him what I thought about the whole Jonny Freeman situation. "But, Captain Greenberg, he kept saying that Carmen had cursed him and that he deserved it. He said he felt as if he had been damned. He said he thought he was already in hell. He said he just wanted to die."

"What did you think when he said he thought he deserved it?"

"Well, I thought he was confessing. That he deserved to be in hell because he had hurt Carmen."

"Could you try to write down everything you remember?"

"Yes. I'm sorry, I was in such shock by the whole experience I forgot to write anything down."

"Just write it down now, if you can, while it's still fresh in your mind. E-mail it to me when you finish, all right?"

"Yes. I'll do that. But I have something more." I was biting my lip, because I wasn't sure how he would take the next bit.

"What is it?"

"I saw the coach and Luke Skywalker there."

"Did they see you?"

"I don't know. I saw them when I was getting into the elevator and they were coming out of the other elevator on the burn unit floor, but I don't think they saw me. Only, I can't be sure."

"That doesn't sound good. Listen, Lucy, be extra careful now. Stay with Seth or one of your other friends whenever you leave the house. Ride with someone to school. Do you have a friend you can ride with?"

"Yes, I have my friend, Wendy, from down the street."

"You had better start carpooling with her. Do you think she'll be okay with that?"

"Yes. She'll understand." I didn't tell him Wendy had come with me to the hospital. I didn't know why, and I guessed it didn't matter, but he did sound genuinely concerned.

"Don't forget about that e-mail."

"I won't." We said our good nights, and I wrote whatever I could remember in an e-mail and sent it to Captain Greenberg before I called Seth.

That night, I was too keyed up to sleep again, so even after taking a Valium, I sat around in the rumpus room watching, or trying to watch, some old movies until well past 2:00 a.m. That's why I heard the shuffling of feet upstairs and the front door closing. My own room extended out from the house and was built under the back deck, with its own en suite, so people weren't usually moving about above my head, but the rumpus room was directly under the entrance to the house.

I knew it was my dad leaving. He was a heart transplant surgeon and was often called out in the middle of the night. He had to be on call whenever a heart became available. He was one of the experts in his field, so even when we were on holiday, like in Europe last summer, he would go jetting off for a few days to pick up a heart for someone. They called it harvesting. He also harvested other healthy organs people might want to donate, like livers and kidneys, but he was mainly renowned for his ability to remove hearts from freshly dead or comatose donors. Anyway, it wasn't unusual for him to leave the house in the early hours of the morning, so I didn't think anything more about it except to feel sorry for him having to get out of his comfy bed.

He didn't get back home until the next morning, Sunday, when we were all in the breakfast room feasting on Constanza's huevos rancheros. He was weary but hungry after his long night, so he joined us. That was how I heard the news about Jonny Freeman so quickly.

"Where have you been?" my mother asked him.

"I've been working on a fellow student of Lucy's," my dad answered. And I knew right away he was talking about Jonny. My appetite evaporated, and I began to feel sick with guilt. Had my visit caused his death somehow?

"It was that boy that crashed his car off Bellagio last year, the one with all the horrific burns. It looks like his body rejected the last skin grafts, and he had some toxic reaction and died in the middle of the night."

Constanza put down a huge plate of Mexican eggs in front of him, but he kept on talking even as he dug in. "Actually, his doctors thought he had finally lost the will to live. The nurses reported him slipping into a coma around 1:00 a.m., and that's when they called me. Jonny's parents had signed the donor papers during the first week of his hospital stay, donating any of his undamaged and healthy organs. He still had a good heart, a healthy liver, and one good kidney."

"Oh, the poor boy!" sighed Constanza, listening to my dad as she heated up more of her tortillas.

"Yes, his injuries had been so extensive it was a wonder he had survived at all. His doctors told me that when his injuries began to heal enough for the burn surgeons to work on rehabilitating him, it became evident that he was extremely depressed, although that wasn't surprising in cases like his. Nevertheless, it only slowed down his recovery further."

I didn't say anything, but I listened carefully, and I could only believe it was my visit that had sent him over the edge. He had certainly been weeping when I left him. But then the coach and Skywalker had visited him after me, and they had seen me leave his ward. Could they have done something to cause his death?

I must have looked pretty sick because my dad tried to comfort me. "Don't be sad, Lucy. At least his death ended his misery, and the donation of his organs saved a lot of other people from miserable deaths."

"What happens to his body now?" I asked.

"Well, under the circumstances, an autopsy was deemed unnecessary. His parents had his body taken to Forest Lawn Cemetery after the surgery. He's being cremated this morning. They'll be holding a memorial service for him later this week. I think they're just glad it's all over."

"It's just so sad!" was all I could muster, and I stumbled from the table and hurried to my room to e-mail Captain Greenberg and telephone Seth.

CHAPTER 27
LET'S HEAR IT FROM THE CHEERLEADERS

AS SOON as I was finished giving Seth the rundown of my day, I called Wendy. I needed to call her because I was going to do exactly what Seth's father told me to do, and that meant recruiting Wendy to be my chaperone whenever Seth wasn't available. She was delighted, just as I thought she would be, and she came over that Sunday afternoon, and we talked some more about the cheerleading squad and how she should approach her friend Caroline and get her to tell her what was really going on.

By that time, Caroline had already quit the cheerleading team—right in the middle of the season. The reason she gave was that it was affecting her grade point average, and she wanted to get into Stanford. She had also stopped hanging out with the other girls on the squad and joined the chess club instead! She remained friends with Wendy, but she stuck to her story about the routines being too difficult and how the practices were interfering with her studies. She still looked haggard and depressed, and Wendy said she thought Caroline had lost about twenty pounds since joining the squad.

Right then, it looked like Wendy was Caroline's only friend. So, what the heck, we decided she should call her right from my room and see if Caroline wanted to hang out with Wendy. As we suspected, Caroline seemed desperate to have Wendy's company, and they made a date to meet up after school on Monday. We had to navigate around the buddy system, so we agreed Wendy would bring Caroline to her house, and we roped in Wendy's mother to drive Caroline home afterward.

Now, we just had to get through the school day in one piece, and I was feeling pretty shaky about walking the school corridors alone, so the next morning, Wendy drove me to school, and we met Seth in the school parking lot as usual. Everything seemed peaceful enough, and the day went pretty much like any other day. We just stuck closer together than we usually did, and Wendy joined me in my free periods in the seniors' lounge whenever Seth wasn't there. We all kept texting each other our whereabouts, but as the day wore on, I felt pretty safe, though I worried about Seth's baseball practice and his situation in the boys' locker room.

Wendy and I had scraped together one hundred dollars from our spring clothing allowance to give to Seth for the steroids in case Carl approached him again. It seemed like the wisest plan of action if we were to keep him from looking suspicious or like a Goody Two-shoes. I made him promise to phone me as soon as he was safely out of there and on his way home.

Wendy drove me home along with Caroline, and we chatted casually about our future school choices and didn't bring up anything that was actually on our minds. I had to admit that, although I didn't know Caroline at all, I would never have pegged her for a cheerleader. She was very thin and pale, with long, straight dark hair, a pleasant face, and a pretty but furtive smile. She looked nervous, as if she were ready to leap out of the car at any moment and seemed totally devoid of confidence.

While I waited for Seth to call me, I played mindless word games on my phone. When he finally did, it turned out everything was perfectly normal at the practice and in the locker room. Nobody paid any particular attention to him except to swoon over his fantastic curveball. And he deliberately left early before Carl Brandt could offer him any drugs. I promised to phone him back as soon as I heard anything from Wendy, and then I watched some reruns of *Boston Legal* and didn't do any homework until I got her text at around 10:00 p.m.

She was coming over in person to talk me to me, after her mother drove Caroline home. Her mother walked Wendy to our door, and my mother actually promised to drive Wendy back home again, even though she only lived five houses away; that's how happy everyone was to see us being friends and how worried everyone was about the murders.

Wendy and I grabbed a couple of Diet Cokes from the fridge and ran down to my room. She sat across from me, on the bed Carmen used to lie on, and before I could even ask a question, she began.

"Oh, Lucy, it's even worse than we could have imagined! Caroline told me that after Coach Billy came to the school, the cheerleading squad tryouts changed drastically. They still had the three weeks of intense practice, where everyone who wanted to be on the squad had to learn one routine, and they still had to choreograph their own routine and perform it for the final tryouts. But after that, it got ugly."

"What do you mean?" I asked.

"Normally, the final tryouts consisted of how well they performed that one routine and how original their own routine was. After that, each of the finalists was interviewed by the captain of the squad and the captain of the football team, followed by an interview with the coach. The difference this year was that the interview with the coach was a private interview, held in his office behind locked doors!"

"No!" I exclaimed, feeling a familiar nausea coming on.

"Yes. You can imagine what that meant," Wendy said, looking horrified. "It turned out in order to make the squad, you had to perform oral sex on the coach!"

"Oh my God," I gasped. "I knew it! What a disgusting creep!" Coach Billy was not the most attractive of men, and no girl in her right mind wanted to give him any sexual favors, but girls trying out to be cheerleaders weren't really in their right minds, and it must have seemed to most of them that a little blow job was the least of all the favors he could ask of them.

"Yes, it sounds totally repulsive," agreed Wendy, "but they all did it, even Caroline. Afterward, she was thoroughly disgusted with herself. She said it was the most revolting experience she'd ever had, and she barely made it out of the coach's office before throwing up."

"That poor girl! But how could she go through with it?"

"I don't know. It sounded worse than you can imagine. She told me that he held her head so hard she thought she would strangle, and that he kept calling her a stupid bitch and that he laughed when he came."

"Just hearing about it makes me want to throw up," I said.

"Still, when it was over, she was on the team. At first, she just hated herself, but then she thought being on the team would be worth it. She said none of the other girls ever spoke about it, and so she never said anything either, and that seemed to be the end of it."

"But it wasn't, was it?"

"No, not by a long shot. Afterward, it turned out, as the semester progressed, the coach began to demand more sexual favors from the girls before every game."

"His pound of flesh," I said, totally nauseated now.

"Exactly. Plus he preferred a nice rotation of girls, and what was even worse was now he expected full-on intercourse in the privacy of his office."

"But how could they stand for that?"

"It seems like even though all the girls were upset by this, so much so that they finally began to confide in each other, the head of the squad,

Alyssa Bachman, that blonde bitch who made it to captain by putting out
for the entire football team, wouldn't let any girl escape her little duty to
the coach. Nobody wanted to quit the squad, and they were afraid that if
they came forward, everyone would know how low they had sunk to get
on the squad in the first place."

"So they were trapped into sinking even lower," I said.

"Yes, it was totally repulsive. Caroline hadn't had her turn with the coach
yet, but she began to hear all the stories. The girls complained about how awful
he was. He hurt them if they didn't give him what he wanted. That's when all
those injuries started turning up. Natalie told Caroline that he bent her over his
desk and started spanking her, and when she resisted, he punched her. That's
how she got the black eye. She said resistance only seemed to make him more
excited and he could hardly get it inside her fast enough before he came."

"This gets more and more revolting," I said, my head spinning.

"When it was Caroline's turn to meet with the coach, she tried to get
out of it and made quite a scene outside his office, but the squad captain
forced her to go in. She told her that if she didn't do it, she would tell
everyone in the school what Caroline had done to get on the squad."

"That must have been the scene Seth witnessed from the batter's
box!" I said. "It looked really suspicious to him at the time. Poor Caroline."

"Caroline said that as soon as she walked through the door, the coach
came up behind her and locked the door. He already had his thing out and was
rubbing it against her backside. Then he began laughing and groping her
breasts from behind, pushing her across the room the whole time. She said he
slammed her face down on his desk, lifted up her skirt, pulled down her
panties, and started pinching and slapping her bottom, calling her a stupid bitch
the whole time. Caroline simply couldn't take it. When he began to spread her
cheeks, she knew she couldn't let him. That was all there was to it. She twisted
out of his grasp, kneed him with her bony knee, and made it to the door."

"Good for her!"

"While he was writhing on the floor, clutching his balls and cursing
her, she managed to unlock the door and escaped into the gym, pulling up
her panties before anyone saw her."

"She's lucky she escaped," I said.

"Lucky and brave," agreed Wendy, "but she was so shaken she couldn't
face the squad captain after that, so she announced that she quit in a text and
then stayed home from school with a 'sore throat' for the following week."

"She must have been terrified that her parents would find out."

"She did talk to some of the other injured girls on the squad afterwards and they were all supportive, but they were still too scared to do anything. No one wanted to come forward and tell the authorities what was going on. They were all too embarrassed, and most of all, they didn't want their parents or their boyfriends to know how low they had sunk."

"I've got to admit, that would be difficult, but how could they let it happen in the first place?"

"It's just high school peer pressure, Lucy. Every girl except you and me wished they could be a cheerleader," said Wendy. I looked at Wendy and realized then that she would have made a great cheerleader, but she had never been interested in any of it. I suddenly felt a new respect for Wendy growing inside me.

"Poor Caroline," I said again.

"Oh, it was awful just listening to her tell me about it. She cried the whole time, and she made me swear that I would never tell another soul."

"And then you came right over here to tell me!"

"That coach is evil. He has to be stopped," she said decisively.

"You're right. We've got to do something," I agreed.

"But what?" asked Wendy. "Caroline's never going to testify. She'd rather die than let her parents find out what she did!"

"Listen, Wendy. She has no choice. She's just like any other victim of abuse, and this is exactly the way all predators keep their victims under control. The victims are too ashamed to tell anyone. It's up to us. Even if I didn't think the coach was a brutal murderer already, I would still take this information to the authorities."

"But, I promised her I wouldn't tell anyone...."

"It will be okay," I said, making it up as I went along. "She might never have to testify, and it might not even have to come out publicly. I'll talk to Seth first—and then I'll call Seth's dad. It might just be all the evidence he needs to get a warrant or whatever to arrest the coach, and if the coach is the murdering motherfucker I think he is, the cheerleaders won't need to testify. They'll get his DNA after they pick him up!" I think I'd watched enough CSI and Law and Order to believe what I was saying.

Anyway, I convinced myself. I felt as if we had more ammunition now, and that disgusting creep was in our sights.

CHAPTER 28
THE HUMMER

IT WAS late already, so we asked my mom if it was okay if Wendy spent the night. Of course it was all right, but we had to ask anyway. I had two single beds in my room and lots of clothes in my closet, so while I called Seth, Wendy told her mom she was sleeping over.

"Yuck!" was the first thing out of Seth's mouth after I told him the ugly story Caroline had related. "But you're right. You should call my dad right away. This is probably all he needs to make an arrest."

"Is he awake? It's midnight already."

"Yeah, he's in his study, working away on this case."

We agreed to talk again after I spoke to his dad so we could figure out a plan for tomorrow. Now that we were getting so close, I was becoming more fearful, and I was glad to have Wendy there with me.

I called Seth's dad's cell phone, and he answered right away.

"Lucy! What are you doing up so late on a school night?"

"I've got something to tell you, and I don't think it can wait."

So I told him everything Caroline had told Wendy. Thankfully, he didn't ask me to repeat anything, but I knew he was taking notes. After I finished, he said, "Well, that's pretty grim news, but it coincides with the information we've been picking up in our own investigation. It turns out that he was quietly retired from his last job at that Midwestern college. There was a stack of accusations against him that they swept under the rug while he was driving their team to success until they couldn't hide it any longer. They were finally forced to let him go."

"Gosh, what happened?"

"Seems he was working the same game plan, only there, one of the girls committed suicide. So after their team won their division, they whitewashed the coach and let him go off to your high school as soon as the season was over."

"That's awful. Really awful." That was all I could say because I started to cry, thinking about how this horrible thing shouldn't have happened to Carmen and how she wouldn't have had to die if those jerks at that last school had only had the guts to charge the coach.

"Look, Lucy. We've got enough evidence now, not just from the sexual misconduct, but we've narrowed down that list of vehicles I told you about. We ran the list the school gave us through DMV to get all the vehicles registered to the students and teachers, as well as those registered to parents of students, and we were able to narrow down the list to just three possible suspects, two teachers, and the coach, but the only vehicle large enough and with the right tires is the coach's. He owns a Hummer H2 in Onyx Black."

"I don't remember ever seeing a Hummer parked in the school lots. He must keep it at his house. I've only seen him driving around in a sporty yellow BMW." But it was chilling knowing he owned such a huge and threatening-looking vehicle.

"The quarterback, Luke Ritter, drives a Corvette, and his pal Carl Brandt drives a Porsche, and we know that Jonny Freeman drove a Lotus. None of their families own large sports vehicles. So it pretty much narrows down our search to the coach's Hummer. But you say he doesn't bring it to the school?"

"No, I've never seen it there. Just his yellow BMW."

"Interesting. That means we can send our forensics team with a warrant to take his car while he's at the high school without him knowing. That's good. It will give us a little safety cushion."

I didn't know exactly what he meant by this or how wrong he was going to prove to be. All I asked was "So do you think you'll be arresting him tomorrow?"

"We'll try to process his car while he's at the school and move in on him before school lets out. You'll stay clear, won't you? Maybe you should plan on leaving school early tomorrow."

"Seth has baseball practice after school."

"Well, I'll make certain he misses that tomorrow."

"Good. I was worried with him being in the same locker room as the football team and all…."

"You just take care of yourself, Lucy. Stay away from the gym, and get home early, promise?"

"Oh yes. I promise."

"Good, because once we move in, there's no telling what will happen."

"Good night, then, sir, and good luck."

"Try to get some sleep."

"I will."

I hung up and immediately telephoned Seth. I was so overcome by terror and excitement I could hardly speak.

"It's all coming down tomorrow!"

"What do you mean?"

"Your dad's going to arrest the coach! You've got to miss baseball practice. You've got to keep away from the boys' locker room."

"Christ!"

"I've got Wendy with me, and we're going to drive to school together, but you and I are going to leave early, understand? We're not going to get involved. It's all too dangerous now."

"I've got it, Lucy. Look, I hear my dad coming upstairs. I'll see you in the usual place tomorrow morning. We'll talk about it then."

I hung up and filled Wendy in on the other half of all the conversations she had overheard. Then we hugged each other and brushed our teeth, and I split a Valium with her so we could both get some sleep.

CHAPTER 29
SETH!

THE NEXT morning, the alarm woke Wendy and me bright and early, although we were pretty groggy from our worry-filled sleep. It may have been a premonition or maybe just foresight, but we chose jeans and sneakers to wear that day, not the kind of outfits we usually wore to high school. We felt like we should be prepared to run. Just in case.

We weren't hungry either, but we each ate everything Constanza set on the breakfast table before us, which included Spanish omelets with avocado and cheese, big glasses of orange juice, and two pieces of toast, with butter yet. Wendy and I were taking pains to be fortified that morning.

Then we whisked down Wilshire Boulevard in Wendy's car and made it to my usual parking spot with twenty minutes to spare before homeroom. I was happy to see Seth's car already there. We leaped out of Wendy's car with smiles of relief on our faces, which faded in seconds. Seth wasn't inside his car, and not only that, his car was unlocked and his book bag was lying on the passenger seat. Foolishly, I started yelling his name.

"Seth, Seth, where are you?"

Then Wendy, who really wasn't as stupid as I made her out to be, grabbed me by the shoulders and said, "Lucy! They must have him! You've got to call his dad, now!"

"Oh my God, oh my God, oh my God," I mumbled over and over, fumbling for my phone. It suddenly looked like a foreign object in my hand, and I could hardly hold it steady, let alone punch in any numbers. Wendy grabbed it out of my hand and scanned the recent calls, found Seth's dad's number from last night, and called it. Then she thrust the phone back into my hand and pressed it to my ear.

"Lucy! What's up? Why are you calling?"

"It's Seth! He's not here."

"What do you mean he's not there? Where is he?"

"His car's here, but he isn't—and I know he isn't in class, because he always waits here for me, and his car was unlocked, and his book bag is sitting on the seat." I was frightened, and I knew I was babbling, but I couldn't help it.

Wendy yelled then, with her head inside Seth's car. "And his keys are still in the ignition!"

"Oh God," Seth's dad said, hearing what Wendy just yelled. "When the team went round to the coach's house, his Hummer was gone." There was a pause, and I could hear Seth's dad talking to the officers near him, and it sounded like he was sending them over to the school.

"Listen, Lucy. Stay right there. Don't go inside the school. I'm sending a team over now. But, Lucy, is there any reason why Seth should be in danger? Any reason the coach would be suspicious of him?"

"It just has to be that they recognized me at the hospital, and everyone here thinks Seth is my boyfriend."

"Then you're in danger too. Are you still with your girlfriend?"

"Yes, she drove me to school."

"Good, then you have her car, not your own?"

"Yes, it's her car."

"Good. Get back into her car and drive it to someplace else in the school lot, not where you usually park. Then lock the doors and stay there until I call you."

"All right."

"We're on it, Lucy. Don't worry." And he hung up, but I could hear the worry in his voice and knew everything was far from all right.

We did exactly as we were told. Wendy and I got back into her car, and she drove around and parked it in the visitor's lot facing the school so we could watch the other students arrive and go to their classes like on any other school day. It wasn't very long before the first police cars began to arrive. They were being discreet and pulled in to the parking lot without any fanfare. Even though they were in their black-and-whites, they didn't have their sirens on, and after they parked, the officers stepped out quietly and strode into the main building as if they had come to give a talk on drugs. They seemed to be heading for the administration offices. I didn't see Seth's dad, but I guessed he was managing everything from headquarters.

Later, when Captain Greenberg told me what really went on inside the coach's Hummer, all I could do was cry. No one should have had to endure the cruelty that poor Seth had to endure.

CHAPTER 30
TICKET TO MEXICO

"HELLO, DADDY'S boy."

Seth had been waiting for me as usual, sitting in his car looking over his physics homework, watching the entrance to the car park. He didn't notice the big black Hummer pulling up behind his car, so he was totally surprised when his car door was suddenly flung open and a large hand wrapped itself around his skinny teenaged neck.

The next moment he was being dragged out of the car by his neck, slammed up against the back of the Hummer, and there was the football coach, big, burly, and very, very angry.

"You didn't think I'd notice you hanging around with your snoopy girlfriend? You didn't think I'd find out that you're the police captain's kid?" He was shaking Seth by the throat while he spat out these words. He already had the back door of his Hummer open, and he lifted Seth effortlessly, one hand still around Seth's neck and the other on Seth's belt, and thrust him into the back, clamping Seth to a side panel with handcuffs he had at the ready.

"There, you go, daddy's boy. Now you're my ticket out of here." Then, for no particular reason, he smashed Seth in the face with his big fist, smacking Seth's skull against the metal panel, and Seth passed out, his crushed nose bleeding down his shirtfront.

It only took the police fifteen minutes to descend on the school, and fifteen minutes later, the school buzzed with the news that they had arrested the school's star quarterback, Luke "Skywalker" Ritter. No one knew anything about the coach. No one had seen him that morning, and there was no sign of him anywhere.

That gave the coach almost an hour's head start from the time he grabbed Seth. He was headed toward the Mexican border, but by then, the captain had an APB on the Hummer—and it was a pretty distinctive automobile, even in Southern California, so it wasn't too long before the helicopters spotted the car racing down the 405 freeway just past Irvine, heading toward the I-5 and San Diego. Seth's dad was in the lead copter, and he was using Luke Ritter's cell phone, so when he dialed the coach's number, he was pretty certain the coach would pick up, and he did.

"What do you want, asshole?" grumbled the coach.

"I want you to pull over and give yourself up."

"Oh, it's you, Daddy. Look, if you want your son alive, you're going to let me get across the Mexican border."

"You've got my son?"

"Oh yes, I certainly do."

"Let me speak to him."

"I'm afraid I can't do that. He seems to be sleeping."

"Is he all right?"

"Oh yeah. Your baby's just fine. Now, pull your guys off and let me go on through, if you want him to stay that way." By then, numerous highway patrol cars were entering the freeway behind the Hummer, and it looked like he was some kind of celebrity with a police escort.

"No deal. You let my son out first—and alive, before you cross the border."

"That's your deal? What do you think? I'm crazy? I'll drop your boy off in Tijuana after I cross the border, and if you want him alive, I don't want any funny business with the border patrol. You call ahead and have them let me through in one of your special law enforcement lanes. I'm not stopping until I'm past the border, then I'll let your boy out."

"Unharmed."

"Well, you know it's kind of bumpy riding back there."

Seth must have woken up then, because Captain Greenberg heard something that sounded like a groan and then "Shut up back there. Can't you see I'm on the phone? See, Captain, your boy's just fine. Do we have a deal? 'Cause I'm gonna have to merge onto this next freeway, and your patrol cars are in my way."

"You know this isn't going to work. You should give yourself up. Pull over now."

"Look, Daddy, if you want your little boy back home safe and sound, I suggest you just do as I say. How about that?"

"All right. Let me have a minute. I'll keep the patrol cars back. I can see you heading toward the I-5. We'll keep tabs on you, but we won't try to stop you."

Seth's dad hung up, and poor Seth just rattled around in the back of the Hummer. He wasn't gagged, so he tried to reason with the coach, but the coach had attached his handcuffs to the side of the Hummer, just close enough so he could reach his arm around and punch Seth whenever he wanted. So after a while, Seth shut up and prayed.

Meanwhile, Seth's dad did exactly what the coach asked. He ordered the patrol cars to continue to escort the Hummer to the Mexican border without any interference and to pull back as soon as the border patrol was in sight. He called the governor's office and the border patrol arranged for the Hummer to pass through the border without stopping and made no attempt to interfere with the coach's vehicle. Then he called some old friends of his from Texas narcotics who used to work undercover in Tijuana.

CHAPTER 31
THE ARREST

WENDY AND I had been dutifully waiting in her car all this time, watching the change rapidly taking place at our school. Students suddenly began milling around the common areas, and no one seemed to be going to class. Then eight policemen marched our way from the direction of the gym. In the middle of the police group and towering above them all was Luke Ritter. With all the melee going on around him, he looked strangely subdued. His head was bowed, and he just shuffled along, surrounded by the entourage of police officers; gone was his usual swagger and that cocky grin.

"Let's take a closer look. I'm sure it's safe now!" I said to Wendy as I bounded out of the car. I wanted to see him close up.

A mass of bewildered high school kids were following close behind them, but we were already in front and had the best view. I ambled as close to the police cars as possible. Sure enough, I could tell Luke's hands were cuffed behind him, and it actually looked like he had been crying.

Wow, I thought to myself as they opened a police car door and made him lower his head, like they do, so he wouldn't bump it getting in. Four of the policemen kept the crowd back, but I could see the vice principal moving forward, shaking his head with a look of befuddlement on his face. And that's when my phone rang.

It was Seth's dad. "Lucy, we've arrested Luke Ritter at the school, and I think you'll be safe now."

"Yes, I can see. It's happening now. We're watching them drive him away as we speak. But where's Seth? Did you arrest the coach?"

Seth's dad made a barely audible sigh because there was so much wind noise in his helicopter and shouting in the background. "The coach has Seth."

"Oh no!"

"He's got him with him in the Hummer. I'm in a police helicopter just above his van, but I'm going to have to let him cross over into Mexico. He promises to let Seth go after he crosses the border."

"Oh my God, is Seth all right?"

"I think so. I certainly hope so. Listen, I just thought I'd let you know. I've got to go now. They're almost at the border now. Be safe!" And he hung up.

"The coach has Seth!" I said to Wendy, but I was already crying, remembering the horrifying photographs from the autopsies we'd seen and hoping Seth wouldn't share the same fate as my beloved Carmen.

"Oh, Lucy, that's awful. Please don't cry. I'm sure he'll be all right!"

"He's a hostage now," I managed to say between sobs. "The coach is using him to get into Mexico. But there's no telling what he might do to him—or what he might have already done to him. He's a monster."

Wendy put her arm around me and led me back to her car. We didn't even bother checking in at the school. It was pretty much mayhem out there, anyway. And I just wanted to get home. Maybe there would be something on TV about it. I was so worried for Seth. He knew the brutality the coach was capable of. Poor Seth must have been terrified for his own life. I had no idea at the time that he was already bruised and bleeding, handcuffed to the back of the coach's Hummer.

"Let's go to Angela's house," I suggested, after we ducked back into her car. I had stopped crying now, and I could think again. "She should know what's going on, if she doesn't already. We might as well let her know and we can watch the news on the TV from her house. We can call our moms from there."

"Okay," said Wendy, and we streaked out of the parking lot behind the police cars, heading back up Wilshire to Bel Air.

It seemed like ages since I last saw Angela, but it was really only a few days. Still, she was completely surprised to see the two of us outside her front door in the middle of a school day. That didn't stop her from greeting us with her usual warm Southern hospitality, and I filled her in as I led Wendy down the hall to their familiar living room and turned on the TV; I had been a fixture in the house for so long, it was like a second home to me.

"Oh, Lucy," Angela said, "I don't know whether to be happy or sad. It's so good to know they've arrested someone, so now we can finally find out the truth, but your poor friend, I just hope he'll be all right. Poor Captain Greenberg. This is just crazy!"

The local TV stations had already picked up the story. Channel Four's "Eye in the Sky" helicopter was following the police helicopter with Captain Greenberg inside, and they already had downloads from kids' cell phones showing the arrest of Luke "Skywalker" Ritter at the school. It looked like the police had just strolled into his homeroom class and walked out with him. He didn't put up any resistance. It was as if he had been expecting it.

The Eye in the Sky helicopter showed the coach's Hummer as it approached the Mexican border. You could see all the black-and-white patrol cars pulling over before they got to the border. Ahead of them was a line of border-patrol vehicles that seemed to be guarding an opening for the coach to drive through. It was on the very right-hand lane alongside the border-patrol building, but no barricades were up, and we watched in amazement as the Hummer drove right on through.

They were in Mexico.

CHAPTER 32
THE DUMP SITE

"ALL RIGHT, Boehm. You've got what you wanted. Let my son go now."

"Just hold on a minute, Daddy. Don't be impatient. I need to put a few more miles between me and the border."

"I've kept my promise."

"And I'm not in Tijuana yet."

Captain Greenberg thought he heard some muffled groans over the noise of his helicopter, which was now hovering back over the border.

He heard the coach shout, "Shut up back there." Then he thought he heard a thumping noise, and the phone line suddenly got quieter.

"You better not have hurt my son!"

"Don't you worry. Daddy's boy is just a bit of a baby, aren't you, kid?" There was another groan and a thud, which was much more audible now. It took all of Captain Greenberg's self-control to keep from ordering an attack at that moment, but he knew he had to be patient, and all he could do was hope for some tiny shred of mercy or decency at the core of this man; there was no alternative. He had to wait.

Operatives in unmarked cars followed lazily behind the Hummer, reporting its progress, and then, just before the Tijuana city limits, they watched while the coach pulled the Hummer over. He got out of the car, opened the back door, and climbed into the Hummer. He uncuffed an unconscious Seth and literally kicked Seth out the back door. Then he jumped down beside him, and gave the unconscious boy a few more kicks for good measure. The operatives had to sit back helplessly and watch as the coach opened his fly and took a leak all over Seth's back. A few seconds later, they watched him get back into the Hummer and head toward Tijuana. Then they moved in to rescue Seth, radioing for the ambulance that was already waiting at the border.

CHAPTER 33

GETTING HIS OWN BACK

CAPTAIN GREENBERG received the report from his men at the border right after they radioed for the ambulance. Seth was alive but severely battered, with several broken ribs and a broken nose; he was a sorry sight and in a lot of pain, but he would recover. They'd taken him to Scripps Mercy Hospital in San Diego. Seth's dad called his wife immediately, and she was already on her way. Then he called me.

"Seth's safe, Lucy. He's all right."

"He isn't hurt? He's okay?"

"He's a little worse for wear, but he'll be okay. He's already in the hospital in San Diego. His mother's on her way down there now." Even over the clamor inside his helicopter, I could hear the relief in his voice.

"God. I'm so relieved," I said, and tears were already flowing down my cheeks while Angela and Wendy looked on with big eyes, waiting for the news. "What about the coach? Did you get him?"

"He's in Mexico now. But he won't be for long. I've got men working for me on the other side of the border, Lucy. He's not going to get away with this, believe me. I've got to go now, but I'll let you know when he's in custody. Relax, but if you like, you can call Seth's mother. Do you have her cell phone?"

"Oh yes, thank you. I will, and maybe we'll drive down there to see him if that's all right. Thank you so much for letting me know."

He hung up and let the helicopter take him directly back to headquarters so he could question Luke. On the ride back, he telephoned his Texas undercover buddies, Reuben and Carlos, who were now in Tijuana. They were on the case already and had the coach in their sights.

Later, they gave Captain Greenberg a full report of what transpired in Mexico. This was a report that would never be filed in the case notes, but he told Seth as soon as he was able to sit up and listen, and of course, Seth told me as soon as we had some private time together in the hospital.

The agents spied the coach's conspicuous Hummer parked in a lot behind a big tourist hotel in downtown Tijuana. Cocky as usual, he didn't seem to think he had anything more to fear from the authorities.

That's why he looked completely surprised when the two huge mean-looking Mexicans kicked down his door, overpowered him with an electric shock baton, and tied him to the hotel bed with gaffer tape after taping his mouth shut, of course. While he was unconscious, the two undercover cops repaired the door as best they could, then called down for room service. They gave the steward a substantial tip and drank champagne and ate lobster salad on the coach's tab.

When the coach woke up, he was naturally furious, but the cops were unfazed. Reuben gave him another shock with his baton, a lighter shock this time, just enough to hurt him but not enough to knock him out, and the two agents began to debate the advantages of various kinds of torture: finger breaking, nail pulling, cigarette burning, kneecapping, castration. All in front of a now-terrified coach. Afterward, they took turns beating him with their batons until he passed out again.

While he was unconscious, Carlos went down to the pool for a swim while Reuben kept watch. After his swim, Carlos felt hungry again, so while he took a leisurely shower in the room's commodious en suite, Reuben ordered two club sandwiches from room service. When the coach woke up again, he saw the two men smoking serenely, having just finished their meal. The cigarettes gave him pause, and he tried frantically to wriggle out of the gaffer tape and made sorrowful unintelligible noises behind his gag, so the cops decided it was time to turn him over.

"Sorry, big fella," Reuben said as he shocked the coach back to unconsciousness; then they carefully unwound him from the tape, turned him over, and bound him again, leaving his buttocks free. Then they pulled down his pants.

"God, what a hideous mother!" Carlos grumbled.

"The things we do for Greenberg," Reuben said, shaking his head. Then he went down for a swim while they waited for the coach to regain consciousness.

When Reuben returned, the coach still hadn't woken up, so they checked to make certain he hadn't smothered with his face in the pillow.

He hadn't smothered, but they decided to remove the pillow and placed it under his hips to give themselves a better target.

"What do you think? Should we burn him a bit before the finale?" Carlos asked.

"Absolutely."

"Maybe we should start now. It might wake him up. I'd like to get this over with soon. I told Maria I'd take her to the movies tonight."

"Yeah, okay, Carlos. You're right, it's getting late."

The coach woke up as soon as they stubbed the first cigarette out on his buttocks. He was wriggling around so much it was hard to get a good aim, but they didn't want to knock him out again. Pretty soon the smell of his sizzling flesh became too nauseating, and they had to stop and walk out onto the balcony for some fresh air and to discuss which one of them was going to deliver the finale.

"Jeez, he's so ugly, and it already smells like shit in there."

"We promised the captain."

"Yeah, I know *you* did, Reuben. So, will you do it to him, then?"

"Okay, okay. I'll do the honors. I think you'd better come in too, though. I might need your help."

"Jeez, do I have to?"

"Come on, Carlos. Don't be such a girl."

When they returned to the room, the coach was wriggling around even more frantically and moaning into the mattress. The two men stood on either side of the bed. Reuben had picked up his baton and begun to adjust the charge.

"What do you think? Three or four, maybe?"

"I don't know, Reuben, we don't want to make too much of a mess and we have to get him out of here afterward. Maybe just two. I think he'll get the idea even if you turned off the thing."

"Three, then. The captain wants an experience this piece of shit will never forget." And with these words, Reuben inserted the charged baton into the coach's rectum while Carlos held him down. Even with the gag, the coach's screams were louder than they expected. Reuben shoved the baton in as far as it would go, and the coach passed out.

"I think he got the idea, don't you?" Reuben remarked. He removed the reeking baton and sauntered off to the bathroom to clean up.

The two men had brought along a full-length terrycloth robe, the kind the hotel might have provided for its guests, and after unwrapping the coach from the bed and rewrapping him so that his arms were pinned to his sides, they clothed him in the robe, put a sun hat over him, and injected him with just enough phenobarbital to keep him unconscious while they took him down the service elevator and out to the coach's own Hummer. They drove him back to Los Angeles and parked the Hummer in Silverlake, not too far from police headquarters, and informed Captain Greenberg of the location. Reuben tossed his baton into the nearest dumpster, and they drove back to Mexico.

Later on, Reuben told Captain Greenberg that Carlos made it to the movies that night with Maria. He took her to see *Pulp Fiction*, which Captain Greenberg thought was an interesting choice. Evidently, Maria didn't like it very much.

CHAPTER 34
CONFESSION

"I'M SO sorry about your friend," Angela said, offering me a pretty lace-edged hanky to dry my tears with. "But he's going to be all right. This whole awful ordeal is going to be over at last. And, Lucy, you helped the police solve this. You really did!"

"Yeah, but my help nearly got Seth killed." I felt terrible, yet elated. "Oh, but I'm so glad he's all right." I wiped my eyes and turned to my mom, who had begun rubbing the back of my neck for some unknown motherly reason. "Mom, is it all right if Wendy and I drive down to San Diego to see Seth right away? I can't bear to wait any longer."

Angela had called my mom as soon as we had turned on the news. My mom then called Wendy's mom to reassure her we were both all right. When my mom explained what was happening, Wendy's mom gave permission for Wendy to spend another night with me.

"Are you up for the drive, Wendy?" my mom asked.

"Oh, it's not a problem, Mrs. Linsky. Anything I can do to help, believe me, I don't mind. And I want to see how Seth is too."

It's true. We had all gotten closer in these last few days before the arrest. We were all friends now, and it was nice to have Wendy's support, and her company would be welcome on the long drive down to San Diego.

"We'll take my car, if it's okay, Mom," I said. "It gets better mileage." My car also went a lot faster, and the sooner we got to Seth and I saw for myself that he was all right, the better, but I didn't say that.

"Of course, Lucy," my mom said. "Just don't drive too fast. Seth will still be there, whether you get there thirty minutes later by driving safely or not. Please, Wendy, make sure she obeys the speed limit, okay?"

Wendy assured her we would be as good as gold, and then we ran across the street to my house to pick up our coats and whatever else we might need. It was a shock when we stepped outside into the glare of daylight. I couldn't believe it. It was only one o'clock in the afternoon. How could all this have happened in only the few hours since breakfast?

The early hour turned out to be a good thing now, because it meant we could make pretty good time on the San Diego Freeway—the 405—and there was an entrance and an exit close to my house. I'd been avoiding these ever since Carmen disappeared. I never took that exit anymore, the one next to Frank Sinatra Jr.'s telephone booth, the one closest to the last place Carmen still lived and breathed.

I kept those memories on the back burner and tried to keep my speed under control as we headed down the freeway, but I was so anxious to get there, it was all a blur. I just turned up the stereo and listened to Ladytron's gorgeous electronica harmonies, and then, before I knew it, we were at the outskirts of San Diego. I turned down the stereo while Wendy used her phone to google map the way to the hospital, but after only a few wrong turns, I managed to find it and drove right to the emergency entrance and parked in the short-stay parking lot there, not caring if I got a ticket or not, just wanting to get inside as quickly as possible and see Seth.

The emergency staff informed us he had already been brought up to a room on the orthopedics floor, and I feared the worst for him, wondering how many broken bones he had suffered.

We raced to the elevator, found the right floor, and made our way to his room. There was a cop stationed outside his door, and I worried for a moment whether they had really got the coach in custody, but when I told the officer who I was, he smiled at me in such a way I realized that he was only there as a favor to the captain. Then he opened the door and let us in.

Seth was out cold when we entered, and gosh, he looked awful. His face was all bandaged up, almost like Jonny Freeman's, and where there weren't bandages I could see how black-and-blue he was. His eyes were so puffy they would have been swollen shut even if he hadn't been asleep. He had one arm in a sling and a small wrist cast on it, and both arms below his hospital gown were swollen and as black-and-blue as his face. He was a heartbreaking sight.

Mrs. Greenberg was sitting in one of the guest chairs and looked up from her magazine as soon as we entered. "Oh, Lucy! I'm so glad to meet you." She got up and hugged me, and I introduced her to Wendy, who had actually started to cry, much to my surprise. She'd been so strong up until now, my rock during this morning's ordeal.

"Oh, poor Seth. How bad is it?" she asked for both of us.

"Well, he's got several broken ribs, but they're all taped up now, a broken wrist, and a broken nose, which he'll have to have set when the bruising on his face quiets down. He's pretty much bruised all over, but the doctors say his internal organs are intact. He looks bad, but he feels worse. When he wakes up, he can tell you all about it. He didn't want to tell me too much, because I'm only his mother. I know it must have been a terrifying experience." Then she gritted her teeth and spat out the next sentence. "If I could get my hands on that monster, I'd kill him myself."

With these words, Seth opened up his swollen eyes as far as he could and tried to smile. "Lucy!" he called out. It was only a whisper, really, but I could hear the excitement in his voice.

Wendy and I rushed over to his bedside, and Mrs. Greenberg stood back and simply observed our sorry little reunion. "What's the idea, going for a ride in the coach's Hummer without me?" I joked.

"Yeah," Seth sighed. "It was a real joyride."

"How bad was it?" Wendy again asked the question that was on my mind.

"It was worse than anything you can imagine," Seth answered, groaning as he tried to turn his face away. But that was obviously too painful a position, so he just groaned again and turned back so he could look up at us through his swollen eyelids. "Basically, I thought I was going to die. He just kept hitting me and hitting me, but the worst thing was knowing all the time that he was going to kill me anyway. I still don't know why he didn't."

"Your dad made a bargain with him," I told Seth. "If he let you go, he'd let the coach escape to Mexico."

Seth made a painful grimace. "Does that mean he goes free?"

"I don't think so. Your dad has some kind of a plan. Now that you're safe, he's got something in the works down in Tijuana. He doesn't seem worried about it. He's pretty certain he's got the coach. He's going to call me when he has him in custody, but he sounded really sure about it."

"I hope so," Seth moaned. "I hope so. That creep can't be allowed out there. You should have seen him, Lucy. He was so ugly. So crazy and mean." Seth groaned again from the effort it took to talk. "God, I hurt all over."

"Would you like some more pain medication?" his mother asked. She had crept up behind us while we talked.

"Yes, actually, I would, Mom," he answered. "You don't mind, do you, Wendy? Lucy? I'm gonna take something, and it's going to make me pass out, but just for a little while. I'll feel better when I wake up."

"No, no," Wendy answered, "we don't mind."

"You won't go away, will you? You'll stay here, won't you? I'll just fall asleep for a few minutes, and then I'll wake up again, and it would be nice if you were still here."

"Of course," I assured him. "We'll wait with your mom. Your dad will call soon, and we'll all still be right here." I moved out of the way for the nurse, who came in with Seth's mom. She injected something into the IV tube running into Seth's arm.

Sure enough, in a few seconds, Seth's eyes glazed over, and he nodded off. The nice officer from outside came in with some chairs for Wendy and me, and we sat down.

"Would you girls like a coffee? I'm going down to the cafeteria, and I can bring you back something," Mrs. Greenberg asked kindly.

"Yes, that would be great," I answered. "Black coffee would be wonderful for me."

"Milk and two sugars for me, please," called Wendy as Mrs. Greenberg turned to go.

For a while, Wendy and I joked about the possible new nose Seth was likely to get, and then Mrs. Greenberg returned with our coffee and some pastries, and we sat and made small talk about school while we ate.

Later I heard that back at police headquarters, Captain Greenberg was sitting with a very morose and acquiescent former star quarterback. They were in the interrogation room in the felony wing of the county jail, and Captain Greenberg had been questioning the quarterback for over two hours. Luke held nothing back, and only his weeping interrupted his confession, and later, after Seth was released from the hospital and returned home, where he had access to his computer once more, he downloaded the transcript and brought it over to my house so that he, Wendy, and I could read the whole sorry thing.

"I want to come clean," Luke had said right away. "I've got nothing left to hide. I know my life is over. Everything I worked for since I was a kid. I know it's all over now.

"I always knew I would be a great quarterback, ever since I was a kid, but the Uni High team was crap until Coach Billy came along. He built up the team and promised to make me a star. That's exactly what he did too. Every major university scouted me last year. I could take my pick of any college in the USA. They all offered me a full scholarship. I knew it was only a matter of time before I made it into professional football.

"But that's all over now. Coach Billy was working too many angles. I knew something was wrong, but he kept telling me what a star I was going to be and how I just had to stick to the program, and the world would be mine.

"But then everything got weird. All last year, I felt like I was on a roller-coaster ride. Everything was out of control. I felt like I couldn't control anything in my life except the football. When I was on the field, I felt good, sure of myself, sure of my team. But then I started having these nightmares. About that girl, Carmen. I knew that somehow I was involved in her death, but I didn't know how. I couldn't remember. But I kept having these dreams, and they seemed so real.

"Later, I began to remember things. I remembered being very, very drunk that Wednesday afternoon, the same day that girl was killed. Coach Billy had invited me over to his house that day after school. We didn't have practice, so we sat around drinking all afternoon. I remembered that Jonny Freeman was there too. Jonny was a funny guy, nice to have around. Too bad what happened to him.

"Anyway, we were all drunk, and then the coach said he had some MDMA, so Jonny and I had some of that too. Then he had some other pills. I thought he said it was speed, but he must have slipped us a Viagra tablet, because later on I got this god-awful erection that wouldn't go away. But I was so drunk and woozy from the MDMA, I couldn't feel a thing, and after that it was all a haze.

"I remember driving around in the coach's Hummer, high as a kite. Then something horrible was happening. I know I was part of it, but it was like a dream. It wasn't really me doing it, because I couldn't feel anything. It couldn't have been me. But Jonny was there, and that girl, and we were all doing something really bad to her, because she was screaming. But the coach had the music turned up, and I thought it must be the stereo. I still couldn't feel anything, and my vision was all blurry. It was like it was all happening to someone else. Like I was watching a bad movie or something.

"I remember seeing Coach Billy doing something I knew was wrong, but I don't remember exactly what it was. All I remember was that it made me feel sick watching him. But all the time I had this enormous erection that wouldn't go away. No matter what I did, I couldn't make it go away. Then the coach must have driven me back to the school locker room, because I remember him putting me in the shower, and somewhere along the line, I lost all my clothes. I only remember waking up in my bed the next morning, stark naked and with a terrible headache.

"When I heard about the murder, I knew deep down that I was somehow involved. I went to the coach and asked him if he knew what was going on. The coach told me I had dreamed the whole thing, but that I'd better not say anything about it or it would ruin my football career forever.

"I thought that was a weird thing to say. I knew something wasn't right, but I pretended that it really was all a nightmare, a dream. It hadn't really happened. But deep down, I knew, especially when it happened the second time, I knew. I just couldn't let myself believe I was part of it. I couldn't let myself believe the coach had anything to do with it. Coach Billy was my friend. He was training me to be a big star. I was going to earn loads of money and show my dad up. I convinced myself it hadn't happened. How could it? I didn't need to rape any girls. Girls loved me; they worshipped at my feet. Well, except for those two.

"Those two girls were different. I remember asking each one of them out for a date. I liked to score the pretty new girls before anyone else got ahold of them, but neither of them was interested in me. That Carmen was so beautiful, and she smiled so sweetly. What a gorgeous mouth. But she still said no to me. And that blonde Viking girl, she was nearly as tall as I am, but she put me down with a nasty comment about my brains, like I was dirt under her feet. I told the coach about them. I just mentioned it. Just saying that some girls in the school thought a little too much of themselves. I hadn't meant to start anything. You have to believe me, I would never hurt those girls."

CHAPTER 35
RESOLUTION

GRADUALLY, MORE and more details of Coach Billy's hold on Luke Ritter came out in the press. After the horrific details of the high school girls' murders, the football team's steroid addiction became front-page news. The school was stripped of its trophies when it was uncovered that the coach had the whole team hooked on steroids and had been selling steroids to wannabe athletes in the regular student body. High on testosterone all of the time, the football players were always ready for a scrap, ready to beat the other teams into a pulp, and were completely beholden to the coach for their success on the field.

"I know I shouldn't be talking to you two about this," Captain Greenwood told Seth and me one night, a few weeks after the arrests. We were sitting in their den, drinking herbal tea that Seth's mom had made us before she tiptoed off to bed, leaving us alone to discuss the case. "But after the parts you both played in all this, I feel you have a right to know. But you mustn't share this with anyone, got it?"

"Got it, Dad," Seth said right away.

"Not even with Carmen's brother?" I asked. "I know he can keep a secret, and he should know what's going on too, don't you think?"

"I've met James," Captain Greenberg said. "I agree he's a solid young man. If you feel that he'll be discreet...."

"Definitely," Seth agreed. I'd brought James to visit Seth in the hospital, and just as I had expected, James had made a great impression.

The captain put down his tea and looked across the coffee table at both of us. "I'm pretty certain that the combination of steroids and alcohol, plus the MDMA and the Viagra the coach slipped Luke, put him into the state the coach wanted him to be in when they kidnapped each of the two girls. Somehow, it must have enhanced his own pleasure to have Luke there to be part of the crimes, but he didn't want him to be too aware of what actually was going on. He probably counted on the drugs making

Luke forget what actually happened. It worked, to a degree. Luke hasn't been able to remember anything clearly, but he's definitely come to believe that the coach raped and murdered both girls. He also believes that he took part in the girls' rapes too, but he honestly can't remember doing it."

"Do you believe him?" I asked.

"I do," Captain Greenberg answered, looking at me, his eyes gray in the den's dim lighting. He looked overwhelmingly sad. "It's the way he talks about it, Lucy. He keeps telling us how sorry he is about everything, and he cries all the time. He says he's sorry for what happened to the girls and sorry that he couldn't remember. Then he starts crying again."

"Is he going to get bail, then, at the next hearing?"

"No, his mental state is too unstable. They've postponed the hearing. The psychiatrists have determined that he is a danger to himself, and they cannot assure the public that he is not a danger to others either."

"Coming off the amount of steroids he was on couldn't have helped," said Seth. "His depression must be monumental."

"Plus he knows his life is ruined," I added.

"That too," Seth agreed. "And he's still only eighteen."

"Right now, he's refusing to eat. Even his parents can't make him eat. We've had him transferred to the Twin Towers Correctional Facility, to their Psychiatric Medical wing."

"Will he be able to stand trial?" I asked.

"He's not going to have to stand trial himself, Lucy," Captain Greenberg said. "The district attorney is letting him plead out so he can be a prosecution witness against the coach as soon as the coach is ready to stand trial."

"But he was part of the murders!" I protested. "He raped those girls too!"

"I know, Lucy," said Captain Greenberg. "But sometimes we have to make compromises in order to get the worst offenders."

"It doesn't seem right," Seth said.

"If it makes you feel any better," Seth's dad said, "Luke is in a really bad way, psychologically. I have reports from the staff at Twin Towers that Luke is raving all the time. He says he can hear Carmen's footsteps walking the corridors day and night. He wakes up screaming every night and told the staff that he can hear her weeping outside his room. They tell me that all *they* can hear is Luke crying in his sleep before he wakes up."

"Well, I'm glad to hear he's suffering, at least," I said grudgingly. "But does this mean that Luke goes free after the coach's trial?"

"Oh no," Captain Greenberg assured me. "That wasn't the deal the DA made. Luke will have to serve more time in a psychiatric facility until he's well enough to be transferred to state prison. Then he'll have to serve up to fifteen years for second-degree murder."

"Thank God," I said, but even after all the horror of Carmen's murder, I had to admit to feeling sorry for Luke. I genuinely believed his story that he had been used by the coach in some sick way.

"Remember, Lucy," Seth added, "Luke is going to suffer even more punishment when he reaches prison, being such a beautiful specimen of young manhood."

"But what about the coach?"

"Yeah," said Seth. "When he gets to prison, he won't be anyone's bitch! I can envision him actually thriving in there, coaching the prison sports teams and raping the newest prisoners and probably dealing drugs!"

"Don't let your imaginations run away with you," Captain Greenberg said. "The charges against the coach are going to be rape and murder with aggravated assault, which calls for the death penalty, and on death row, there will be no perks."

"But prisoners stay on death row forever, making appeal after appeal to stave off execution!" said Seth.

"It's too good for him," I complained. "It's not fair. Carmen didn't have any chance for an appeal. Why should her vicious murderer?"

But even this grim scenario had a way of sorting itself out, for the problem ended up solving itself. It happened like this:

When the coach realized what was in store for him as soon as he recovered from his Mexican adventure to be transferred from LA County Hospital to the Parker Center Jail, he began acting sicker than he actually was. He complained to the doctors of terrible pains in his abdomen, and what with all his histrionics, they believed him.

In fact, they thought he might have suffered some intestinal rupture from his anal rape. They arranged to bring him down to X-ray for an MRI, with a police escort, naturally, but knowing how big the county hospital was and how long and busy the corridors were, crowded with patients and staff all the time, the coach evidently counted on finding an opportunity or *creating* an opportunity for an escape.

Wendy, James, and I were in James's living room watching *Homeland* when Seth called me on my cell. I couldn't believe it when I heard the news. It was too good to be true!

James and Wendy, who had only heard my side of the conversation after immediately muting the TV, anxiously awaited whatever news I had.

"Seth just told me the coach tried to escape from County Hospital!" I told them.

"Oh my God!" said Wendy. "That's terrible!"

"No, it's not," I told her, and I started crying tears of relief again. "It's wonderful."

"What exactly happened?" asked James.

"He tried to beat up his guards on the way to the X-ray and evidently hurt one of them pretty badly and managed to get the guard's gun. Then he threatened to shoot an X-ray technician if they didn't let him leave the hospital."

"Oh God, that's incredible!"

"Yeah, it's incredible. Because in LA County Hospital, they have a million armed cops roaming the halls, and one just walked up behind him and shot him in the back!"

"Oh no, is he dead?"

"That's the best part!" I said, laughing now. "It was a .22 caliber pistol, and it broke his spinal cord and bounced around inside him and did more damage than the damage he was already complaining about."

"Is he going to live?"

"Oh yes," I told them. "The doctors are working on him now. They're going to save his creepy life no matter what they have to do. LA County is fantastic with gunshot wounds. Captain Greenberg says the doctors say he will survive just fine with only one kidney and no spleen. They say he'll probably be paralyzed from the waist down, but he'll still feel pain in the rest of his body. Seth's father says the doctors told him there will be *plenty* of pain after they finish operating on him!"

"That's fantastic!" exclaimed James, hugging me.

Later that night, Seth called to tell me that the operation on the coach had been a success. "Can you believe?" Seth said. "He really is going to be paralyzed!"

"Well I hope he can still feel pain, 'cause I want him to hurt mightily!" I said.

"Oh yeah," Seth said. "My dad says he's in a lot of pain right now. And do you know what's even better?"

"No, what?"

"Now the doctors think there might be too much damage inside him after all. Those little .22 caliber bullets tend to bounce around a lot, nicking organs and bones. Now they're thinking he might not survive more than a few pain-filled weeks."

"That means he'll be dead long before he would have even reached death row, let alone made an appeal."

"I thought that might make you happy," Seth said.

"As long as he's suffering now."

"Good."

"Seth?" I said before he hung up. "I'm not really happy about this, you know. I just feel, I don't know." I paused, because I really didn't know what I meant myself.

"Like it's more justice than you could have hoped for?" Seth finished my thought for me.

"Yes," I answered, feeling so close to Seth right then. He knew me so well. "Yes, that's exactly what I mean. Thank you so much, Seth, and thank your dad for keeping us in the loop."

Luke didn't have to face a trial. He simply spent several months in a hospital for the criminally insane before it was finally determined that he didn't really belong there, but where he had been writing long, heartfelt letters to Angela, James, and myself, telling us how sorry he was and how he was going to devote his life to making up for all the harm he had caused. Unbelievable as it might be, he actually tried to do just that.

When he was finally transferred to a regular prison, he began to study for the priesthood. He still kept writing to Angela, because she actually wrote him back, something I couldn't bring myself to do. He told her he was planning to become a prison chaplain, that he was going to work to help other criminals deal with the deeds they had done and help them make up for their past mistakes. I could almost forgive him now.

Almost.

CHAPTER 36
INTO THE FUTURE

THE SUMMER was drawing to a close when James drove Wendy and me over to Pips in his mom's Cadillac for a last roundup before we split for our respective colleges, or in James's case, for his third year at the Air Force academy in Colorado.

Both Wendy and Seth had developed crushes on James over that summer, especially after seeing him decked out in his new Air Force uniform. He had lost a lot of weight during the two years since Carmen's death, and he did look pretty striking, with his blond hair and piercing blue eyes. When you added his fabulous Southern politesse, he was pretty charismatic, especially as he was so damned intelligent and levelheaded too. If I weren't gay, I might have fallen for him myself, but he still made a heck of a friend, military or not, and he'd always be Carmen's beloved older brother, which is as close as anyone could truly get to my heart.

"So it's true. You're giving up creative writing for law enforcement?" he asked me on the drive over.

"Well, it's not technically 'law enforcement,' it's criminology," I said. "I can get a PhD in it, just like Seth's dad."

"Lucy and Seth are both headed for the University of Maryland," chimed in Wendy. "They get to go back east together!"

"It's got the best department of criminology and criminal justice in the country, very high-minded, I can assure you," I added. "And who says I can't still be a writer while I'm out fighting crime?"

As soon as we entered the coffee shop, we spotted Seth sitting in our favorite booth, grinning his latest wonky grin, the one he had worn ever since his nose was broken. Poor Seth had a new nose now, not so unique and aquiline as the old one but not too ordinary either. His bruises had faded, and he looked pretty good.

We settled ourselves in the booth, James sliding in next to Seth and Wendy scrunching up against his other side, looking up at him with huge, love-filled eyes. I sat on the other side of Seth and gave him a big hug.

"Well, show everyone your prize, Seth," I said after we'd ordered our usual coffees. "Don't hold back."

Seth had won a full scholarship to the University of Maryland with a major in cyber crime. It had helped that his father was the captain of Major Crimes for the LAPD, but he had also received loads of recommendations from every one of his teachers, and I had to admit, he was pretty brilliant and certainly knew his way around a computer. Plus I thought it was pretty spectacular that my very best friend would be coming to the same university as me when I was going to be so far from home for the first time.

Seth pulled out the scholarship acceptance letter he had received and passed it around so we could all take turns admiring it. In it, the university declared how delighted they were to offer such an exceptional student this scholarship, which would pay all his fees, including his accommodations, for his first four years in their new Department of Cyber Crime.

"You two are so lucky, going to the same school. I'm going to be all alone in New York City!" complained Wendy.

"Oh really, alone in New York City. What a bummer!" I laughed.

"Don't worry." James smiled fondly down at Wendy, who was still making with the lost puppy eyes. "We'll all meet back here every holiday." All Wendy could do was bask in his smile and savor his words as if they were a promise of their future engagement.

"Anyway, you are the one who is going to be consumed by your career," I said accusingly. "We'll be lucky to ever see you again, once you get under the limelight," I added.

"Don't say that!" protested Wendy. "I'll never be like one of those people. I'm never going to forget any of you." She turned her puppy eyes on me, and I could see there were actually tears forming at the corners.

"I know, Wendy, I was just joking," I assured her. "I know you're not like one of *those* people."

"Well, it's true," began Seth. "We've been through an awful lot together—"

"Some more than others!" I interjected, still reeling from seeing Seth in the hospital just a few months ago.

"Yes," agreed James. "I think we can safely say we've been through the mill together."

"And if that doesn't bond us forever, nothing will," added Wendy.

"So when you're a big Broadway star, you will always remember us and put us on the guest list for all your shows, right?" said James, putting his arm around Wendy and giving her shoulders a squeeze, which gave her an excuse to wriggle even closer.

Seth looked at me with raised eyebrows and grinned that lopsided grin again. "Okay, then, I think it's time for the blood-brother ritual," he announced.

"Hey, there's been enough bloodshed!" I protested.

"I didn't mean *that* ritual," he said. "I just meant that it was time for us to really promise never to forget how strong we all were together and how we should always be there for each other in the future."

"Oh, Seth," cried Wendy. "That's so sweet! Absolutely! I will never forget you all. And I will never forget how tough we can be. I promise to be tough forever!"

"Boy, and you're going to really need to be tough in the showbiz world. Just think of Madonna!" I reminded her.

"Okay, okay, we get it. So what are we supposed to do now? Clasp hands and swear to never forget?" asked James.

"Sounds good to me," Seth said. So that was what we did. Right there in Pips, in the middle of Westwood Village, in the cold, beating heart of LA. We put our hands on the table and held on to each other for dear life.

"I'll never forget," we all swore.

And we never did.

CHAPTER 37
THE DREAM, PART 2

I HAD that dream one last time.

I was back at the Angelus Rosedale Cemetery. Only, this time Carmen was not only alive, but we were sitting together on a plaid tablecloth under the small grove of palm trees beside her grave, and *James* was with us. We were having a picnic!

Carmen and I were laughing at James because he looked so dismayed at the vegetarian fare in the picnic basket. He kept pulling things out of the basket and groaning.

"Ugh! Tofu hotdogs! Didn't you bring anything for me?"

Carmen was leaning back against her very own gravestone. She looked gorgeous in her little black dress, her supple legs crossed in front of her. She leaned forward and reached into the picnic basket. I was dumbfounded when she pulled out a pistol. "Of course I have, James. Here, this is what you want." She handed the pistol to James, who looked at it as if it were a poisonous snake. But he took it from her anyway, and Carmen turned to me, her dark eyes shining, and winked.

From out of nowhere, music began to play. It was a familiar tune, and I thought I recognized it. Yes, I did! It was "Tara's Theme" from *Gone with the Wind*.

James was staring at Carmen now. I had never seen him look so sad. Not since the funeral at least. "Why now?" he asked her.

"It's a present, silly," she answered, laughing her sultry laugh. She reached over and squeezed my hand. Her touch filled me with longing and love for her.

Just then, a man stepped out from behind one of the palm trees. He was tall with dark hair, and he looked somehow vaguely familiar, but I didn't remember ever seeing him before. He walked up behind James so James couldn't see him, but Carmen did. A dark look of recognition swept over her beautiful face. James was watching her, and he turned around to see what she was looking at.

"Dad!" he exclaimed.

The man ignored him and walked right up to our blanket until he could reach down and take Carmen's hand. He pulled her to her feet, although I was straining to hold her down by her other hand. She surprised me by pulling her hand free of mine. But she gazed back at me, looking strangely cheerful. Then she winked at me again as if we shared some secret.

The music began to get louder, sounding sinister among the tombstones and the palm trees. I watched as the man swept Carmen into his arms and began to dance with her. She didn't struggle but danced with him in a strangely formal way as if she were trying to keep him at a distance, but the man whirled her around, and I knew he was trying to pull her closer.

Carmen threw her head back so her hair swirled around her lovely shoulders, and she looked directly at James. James and I struggled to our feet as we watched the strange dance. I didn't know exactly what was expected of me. The overwhelming creepiness of the spectacle froze me to the spot. Then the man moved his face closer to Carmen's, and I could see he meant to kiss her.

And that's when James walked up to them and put the gun against the man's head. The man turned slightly, and I could see a look of astonishment on his face. Then he shook his head and began to smile. His smile shocked me, because it was so reminiscent of Carmen's smile, and that was when James pulled the trigger.

I woke up with start, sweating and terrified in my familiar bed and for the rest of the night, all I could do was wonder and wonder.

Epilogue
In The End

IN THE end, I decided to never tell James or Angela what Carmen's autopsy report had revealed. I know they must have known what had happened to Carmen, and I didn't want to open up old wounds. I believed they had both suffered enough.

At least Carmen's suffering was over at last. Rumors of her ghost haunting the school gradually faded, and no one ever again reported seeing her ghost walking the corridors of University High School.

She also stopped haunting my dreams, and I was able to sleep once more without having to rely on my mother's supply of Valium. That didn't stop me from missing her terribly, though, or from being angry at the universe for taking her away from me. Not a day went by when I didn't wish I could call her up so I could tell her about all the things that were happening in my life.

I wanted to tell her about Seth and about my change in career. I wanted to tell her how we helped solve her murder! Knowing I could never talk to her again still filled me with rage, but I didn't think that would ever go away, and maybe I didn't want it to. I never wanted to forget Carmen.

I was pretty certain James and I solved the riddle of the little black dress and that her overriding motive was to remind Angela of what she had allowed to happen to Carmen, and at the same time, to remind herself the man who had hurt her was gone forever.

I only wished her little black dress could have served as a shield to protect Carmen from further harm. There were so many things I wished for whenever I thought about Carmen. The one thing I wished, above everything else, was that I could turn back the clock to that beautiful spring day when Carmen walked down to that corner without me. If only I had been there. If only I could have saved Carmen from her fate.

I knew in my heart there was nothing I could have done to save her, but no matter what I told myself, it would always break my heart that her little black dress became her shroud.

LINDA PALUND grew up in a small-town library, hiding from bullies and the rest of the world. She was an ugly duckling and a misfit but always knew she would blossom someday. When that day came, she became a model, then a songwriter, then the leader of a rock-and-roll band. But through all her life's changes, she never stopped being a bookworm and always planned to be a writer.

Today, she is taking all the threads of her life, the weird and the wondrous, the fantastic and the tragic, and weaving them into her novels.

She loves to champion the underdog and hopes her novels will give other misfits the hope that they too will prevail against the odds.

You can read her quirky flash fiction at
http://fictionvictimtoo.blogspot.com

Twitter her at https://twitter.com/auralind

Facebook at https://www.facebook.com/Lindapalund

And write to her at auralind@gmail.com

CPSIA information can be obtained at www.ICGtesting.com
Printed in the USA
BVOW08s2343060714

358224BV00024B/648/P

9 781627 988513